5-11 *

D1539205

A CASE OF PUPPY LOVE

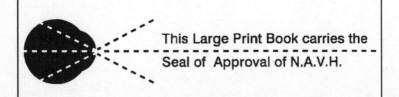

This Large Print Book carries the
Seal of Approval of N.A.V.H.

A CASE OF PUPPY LOVE

LOIS SCHWARTZ

THORNDIKE PRESS
A part of Gale, Cengage Learning

GALE
CENGAGE Learning™

Detroit • New York • San Francisco • New Haven, Conn • Waterville, Maine • London

GALE
CENGAGE Learning™

Copyright© 2010 by Lois Schwartz.
Thorndike Press, a part of Gale, Cengage Learning.

ALL RIGHTS RESERVED
All of the characters in the book are fictitious, and any resemblance to actual persons, living or dead, is purely coincidental.
Thorndike Press® Large Print Gentle Romance.
The text of this Large Print edition is unabridged.
Other aspects of the book may vary from the original edition.
Set in 16 pt. Plantin.

LIBRARY OF CONGRESS CATALOGING-IN-PUBLICATION DATA

Schwartz, Lois, 1939–
   A case of puppy love / by Lois Schwartz.
     p. cm. — (Thorndike Press large print gentle romance)
   ISBN-13: 978-1-4104-3668-9 (hardcover)
   ISBN-10: 1-4104-3668-3 (hardcover)
   1. Single women—Fiction. 2. Triangles (Interpersonal relations)—Fiction. 3. Large type books. I. Title.
PS3619.C4874C37 2011
813'.6—dc22   2011007478

Published in 2011 by arrangement with Thomas Bouregy & Co., Inc.

Printed in the United States of America
1 2 3 4 5 6 7 15 14 13 12 11

To the generous and caring
individuals and organizations that
rescue and comfort abused animals

PROLOGUE

"I already have blankets and a box in the back of the car. I'll be there as fast as I can."

Terri Bookman hung up the phone and ran to dress in old jeans and a sweatshirt. Until the phone had rung, she'd been relaxing in her pajamas in front of the television expecting to turn in after the news. The phone call asking for her help had changed everything.

"I'll be home in a little while," she said to her boys, a white bichon frise and the black toy poodle, who followed her every move thinking that they were going out too. "Can't take you with me tonight, guys, but be good," she added as she tucked a pair of latex gloves into her back pocket. "And remember, the pillows on the couch are not your chew toys."

After a quick look around to see she had everything she would need, she pulled on her washable fleece jacket. Her apartment door locked, she ran down the flight of stairs to the building's exit nearest the parking lot and her car. The well-lit lot right next to the structure was one of the reasons she had chosen an apartment in this building — that and the fact that they allowed dogs.

Checking for the flashlight in the glove compartment before she started her car, she smiled when she found it worked just fine. It had been a couple of months since she'd needed it last because most of her runs had been in daylight hours. One as late as this had to be for something special or she wouldn't have gotten the call so late.

Not more than a twenty-minute drive later, she made her last turn. Once on the right street, finding the place a few blocks down was easy. Red and white lights rotating on top of two police cars illuminated the dingy neighborhood in a steady rhythm of flashes. In the light only when it swung their way, the officers moving around the lawn and driveway looked like characters in an early black-and-white movie, only this one was highlighted in red.

Washed in the same flashes, neighbors stood in quiet groups in their front yards nearby watching the whole procedure. Many of them had donned only a coat or robe to cover their nightclothes. The fuzzy slippers on a few accented the spontaneity of their appearance as spectators. They talked among themselves, and a couple of the women wiped tears from their cheeks at what they were viewing.

The residents of the address to which Terri had been called had already been taken into police custody. They had been locked in the backseats of separate police cars, their loud objections and complaints ignored.

After that the Animal Rescue officers had taken over. Terri was here as a volunteer to help them. She parked in the street behind their van and pulled on her latex gloves before exiting her car. Familiar with the drill, she headed straight to the officer in charge, Sam Martinez, a friend she'd been helping out on such occasions for years.

"What's up?" she asked when she reached his side.

"We've got twenty-seven so far." He pointed to a small ramshackle structure at the back of the driveway where one would expect to see a garage. "Most of them were penned up in there."

The situation was all too common to them both. "We've got the dogs and cats in crates for the drive to the pound, but I don't think some of them will make it. We were making one more sweep through the house when

9

one of the officers heard noises. We discovered some puppies huddling on a pile of dirty clothes in a bedroom closet. That's when I called you," Sam told her.

"They were inside, away from the others?" she asked. "Are they in better shape?"

He shook his head and sighed. "I wish the neighbor had called us sooner," Sam told her. "It may be too late for them, but we have to try."

Preparing to enter the house, Terri took a moment to take a deep breath to fortify herself for the scene she was about to see. If she lived to be a hundred, she would never understand this kind of cruelty to animals, the poor overcrowded housing with not enough food and water — especially when there were newborns.

As she turned toward the front door, Sam stopped her. "Wait — I didn't mean that you had to go in there. I already have the three survivors huddled in a blanket in the truck. My assistant gave them some water. Come on. I'll help you get them to your car."

Smiling with relief she didn't try to hide, Terri followed him to the truck. "I don't know how you do this every day," she said. "And I certainly don't know how people can make their animals live in such conditions, ignoring them to the point of threatening their lives."

"Fortunately, it doesn't happen everyday, but when it does, the neighbors who have to know about it often ignore the situation. That's what I find hard to take. When we finally find the animals, we take care of them the best we can. And thanks to volunteers like you who take the littlest ones, we can save more than we would otherwise."

"And the ones we save make it all worthwhile," she added with a smile. It was an old song but encouraging to say again.

Bent over to keep from hitting his head, Sam stepped up into the back of his Animal Rescue truck. The inside was lined with stacked wire crates containing barking dogs and terrified, silent cats whose huge eyes watched his every move. Passing them, he stopped behind the front seats and bent over a plastic box no bigger than the throw pillows on Terri's couch. Lifting out a blanket and cradling it in his arms, he stepped down from the truck to her side.

Terri lifted back the corner of the wool cover. "They don't look old enough to wean," she said, looking at three very thin and very dirty little puppies.

"From what the neighbor says about their age, they must be close. That gives them a better chance, but after being underfed all their lives, it'll take a while longer," Sam explained as he carried them to her car.

"And what about their mama?" she had to ask.

Sam shook his head. "I don't expect her to make it."

Terri nodded and swallowed past the lump that had lodged in her throat. Concentrating on what she had to do, she blinked away the tears that burned in her eyes. "I'll take good care of these," she assured him as she opened the back of her small SUV to have access to the padded box behind the rear seats.

"With all you've got going, you sure you have time now?" Sam asked.

"You bet," she replied with a smile. "I have customers who are happy to come in just to feed the puppies you give me and help socialize them. I keep a list of their names and phone numbers at home. I'll give them a call in the morning to let them know that I have some now."

"Here you go, little fellas," he said, leaning over to put them in her box. "I'll leave them in the warm blanket. You can return it whenever."

"I'll do that. Thanks, Sam." The puppies installed safely in the car, she and Sam stepped back as he shut the door.

"I'm the one who has to say 'thanks,' Terri. When we're full up at the shelter, I don't know what we'd do without volunteers like you who take in the pups and save their lives. I'm just sorry we had to call you so late this time — late at night for you and late for the pups."

"Oh, that's not a problem. You know I love caring for these little guys, and I'll do my best to prove your prediction wrong."

"I notified the vet, and she'll expect to see them tomorrow."

"Right. Then I'll call in my report to let you know how they're doing."

"Thanks, Terri. Hope you get at least a little sleep tonight," Sam said with a grin.

"Won't be the first time if I don't get much," she replied with a grin of her own.

Terri climbed in behind the driver's seat and didn't hear a sound from the precious cargo in the rear. She had a long night cut out for herself with feeding and cleaning up the pups, but she loved doing it. No matter what the hour, helping to rescue puppies and eventually finding good homes for them gave her a warm, fuzzy feeling every time. She was happy to do it for the dogs and to lighten the load for the people who worked at the dog shelter. They needed all the help

13

they could get.

And it was relatively easy for her to take on several puppies at a time because she could take her new little four-legged friends with her to work each day at K-Nine Treats. There she and her volunteers could care for them during the day instead of leaving them home alone, which would never work.

She couldn't help but keep the smile as she drove home. Life now was looking a whole lot better for the little guys in the back of her car. And after escaping what she'd gone through during her first attempt at business, she was on the road to success at her new location too.

CHAPTER ONE

"Pay attention to where you're going, boys," Terri told her dogs as she jogged in the park at a pace suitable to their short legs. She zipped her sweatshirt higher to block out the cold September air as she ran. "It's almost cold enough this morning to outfit you both in a warm sweater from the store."

K-Nine Treats, Terri's recently reopened shop in a new location in the new Riverside Mall, specialized in freshly baked dog treats and custom-mixed dog food, as well as accessories such as doggy coats, sweaters, and boots. Many of those were custom knit locally and could be ordered in whatever color the customer wanted. The shop was her dream come true. She loved supervising the baking everyday and chose only the best quality of accessories to sell.

Now that the shop was doing well, she could spend some time on herself each morning after she fed the rescued puppies

15

when she had them. She needed to work out her frustration at how the rescued puppies had been cared for, or not cared for, which was more often the case. On some mornings like this one, she needed the brisk, fresh air to reenergize her after being up much of the night with the little guys. So, with the boys on their leather harnesses and leashes, she jogged on the path around the city park pond.

The time outdoors helped keep all their bodies fit, and she liked the time to think through her day and get organized. She'd worked hard on a business strategy that included a plan for every eventuality she could think of. Happy in her new location, she no longer had to worry about a landlord showing up and harassing her. That had been a nightmare at her last shop location downtown. He had showed up more and more frequently. He'd embarrassed her in front of customers with personal comments and made her feel uncomfortable to say the least. When he still tried to get her to go out with him even after she'd refused several times, she knew it was time to move. She'd found the spot in the new mall and was glad to have seen the last of him. She certainly hoped she could trust her new landlord more than the former one.

Her tee shirt advertised her shop in River side with a big dog-treat bone under the shop name. She wore one each morning on her outing with the boys, but this morning was cold enough to hide it under her jacket.

"Oh, no you don't," she had to say more than once when some odor became more interesting to one or both the dogs than jogging. "Away," she commanded sharply as she ran in place. "Run," she added more gently so they would resume their jog.

Pick up the fresh produce for the vegetable bones and more tape for the cash register on the way in this morning, she reminded herself as she watched the asphalt pass the distance between the dogs and her toes. She paid little attention to the joggers coming toward her or passing her at a faster rate from behind.

Wanting to give her boys exercise but not heart attacks, she kept an eye on them to be certain they weren't running too hard. She'd gotten them late in their lives and was working slowly and steadily at getting their weight to a more healthy level. Lapdogs for their previous owner, she liked their mellow, laid-back attitude toward most things — most things, but not other dogs. Ecstatic didn't begin to describe their reaction to meeting a new canine friend. They

17

never met one they didn't love at first sight. She could only imagine that they'd rarely seen other dogs before coming to live with her. At least they were friendly and not confrontational.

Suddenly, the boys veered sharply to the left and pulled her arm with them. Then, stopping, they barked excitedly at a sleek black Labrador beside an oncoming jogger.

But Terri couldn't stop so easily and took a couple more steps past them to recover her balance. Straining at their leashes, the barking boys danced all the way around her and then raced toward the Lab again, tying up her legs in the leashes. She turned and tried to untangle them, but feeling her pull them, the excited dogs charged around her again, adding a second loop around her legs. Jumping up against their shortened leashes toward the Labrador, which was now just a few feet away, they continued to bark happily.

"Sit," she cried to no avail.

The jogger just kept coming. As her dogs lunged toward the large dog, they jerked the straps tight around her knees.

"No. Heel," she commanded.

But the dogs ignored her. Pulling even harder, they tied her legs together tightly. Even trying baby steps failed her. She could no longer maintain her balance. With a cry, she spread out her palms to brace for the fall that seemed inevitable.

Within inches of impact with the rough surface of the path, two strong hands caught her upper arms and pulled her up against a very hard chest.

"Whoa there," he said, laughing. "Are you okay?" Keeping a steadying arm around her, he grabbed the barking boys' leashes and worked to give her some slack. Together, they turned around until she had enough room to step out of the loops and free her legs. Once she was free and standing on her own, he lowered his supportive arm.

"Thanks. I guess I wasn't paying enough attention," she admitted as she quieted the boys with treats after she got them to sit in the heel position. Looking up to see the tall jogger watching her, she remembered the old jacket that she had on and wished she had worn something less disreputable.

With her dogs finally under control, she saw that the sleek black Lab, twice as tall as her pair, was sitting quietly out of their reach. She hadn't even heard the man tell him to do so. Lifting her head, she met the jogger's clear gaze with a new respect for his ability to train his well-behaved dog. Embarrassed, she knew she should do better with the boys, but didn't get a chance to apologize before he spoke.

"I'm sorry if we caused this," the man said, though it had clearly not been his fault. "Fred's home alone all day, so he gets excited when he meets potential new friends," the man explained in a mellow deep voice that would melt the ice in a tall glass of lemonade even on a cool day like today.

Terri had to laugh at his description of his dog. "Fred looks anything but excited. He looks calm and relaxed."

"Yeah, I guess he does. That's why I like this breed," he replied nodding.

"Labs are wonderful, but I didn't have a choice. I inherited mine when they needed a home. As you could guess, we're still working on their behavior," she added with a grin. "The last owner couldn't handle the training, but she made them into very nice people-loving pets."

The deep sound of his laugh resonated in his chest. "You've got your work cut out for you. Have you had them long?"

"No, they've only been with me for a few months. All I need now is more time to work with them. There just haven't been enough hours in each day for me lately."

Stepping back, he reached down and

scratched Fred behind the ears. The dog only spared him a brief loving look that said his thank you, and then his attention was back on the boys.

"I was lucky. Fred was all trained when I got him, so reinforcing his good behavior is easy. He was a service dog for a blind woman. Living as a pet now that he's retired is a new vocation for him."

He picked up the Lab's leash that he had dropped to help her. Fred sat at his side waiting patiently for his next command or for their jog to resume.

For some reason Terri didn't want to jog on, but she knew she had to. "Well, thanks for rescuing me. I think I would have been the loser in the argument with the blacktop path," she said, walking past him and turning backwards to keep the eye contact.

"It was no problem. Have a good one," he said, also turning in order to face in her direction as she moved past him.

"You too," she said as she tugged at the boys' leashes to get them lined up to jog again. "Come on, boys. It's time to go. Run," she commanded. She took a few steps sideways, away from them. Barking a few more times at their new friend, her dogs finally got the idea and ran on ahead of her.

Running after them, Terri wanted to turn

around for one more look at the man's dark hair that fell so invitingly over his forehead. She would no longer be able to see his milk-chocolate brown eyes, but she could still enjoy the broad shoulders and narrow waist framing his smart, new-looking gray jogging suit with a black stripe down each leg. It looked so good with a black tee shirt. And his smile — wow — why didn't she know any men who looked that good?

Sighing, she tried to pick up the pace to work off her disappointment. After having men try to get her name and number when she hadn't wanted to give out the information, she wished the jogger had tried. She just might have given it to him. But he hadn't asked. She could only conclude it was the old clothes she wore, or that he was married or had a steady girlfriend.

The memory of the handsome man remained with her as she jogged home where she showered and dressed for work. Once she had her dogs and the rescued puppies safely caged in the car, she left for the puppies' visit to the vet. Getting a prognosis that all three just might make it, Terri wore a smile as she drove on to work at K-Nine Treats, the most popular spot for dogs and their human companions in Riverside.

After his mid-air catch of the pretty jogger that morning, Carter Morris had waited and watched until she disappeared around the bend in the path with her two little balls of curly fur. Though he jogged every chance he got, he'd never seen her on the jogging path before. From the moment she took off away from him, he'd kicked himself for not asking her name. *That's what all work and no play will do for a guy,* he thought. The past year had been very intense with long hours at work, and he was definitely out of practice.

"If this is what I get for jogging an hour later than usual, I'll have to try it again," he mumbled to himself as he finished his jog and entered his apartment to get cleaned up.

Less than an hour later, with Fred left at home in the kitchen with his bed, food, and toys, Carter walked the half-mile distance along the river to his office at M&S Development Company. He couldn't bring Fred with him today because he had on-site visits. He worried the dog might injure a paw at the construction site. Most days, however, Fred accompanied him to the office.

Dressed in khakis and a cotton shirt, he didn't look like the part owner and the chief architect for all their projects. However, he enjoyed a spacious corner office with big windows in their office building just beyond the park by the river. His partner preferred much richer environs to impress potential rental clients, while Carter needed the office for the light, but he loved the views too.

Looking upstream, he could see the six-foot dam on his side of the Main Street Bridge that sent water rushing down past Riverside, M&S's newest accomplishment. Open for business for less than a year, the shops were always rented and business for them all seemed to be good despite the economy's ups and downs. With all but the final details finished there, he was already designing the next phase of the project, Riverside Two.

Draping his sports jacket, which had doubled as a coat on the brisk morning, around the hanger on the back of his coat rack, he paused a few moments by the windows to enjoy the scenery. Rotating his head after finally sitting down at his desk, he felt pleased to discover the tension that he normally felt there was gone. Getting back to jogging each morning lately had been really beneficial.

"Something must be good. I don't often see you with a smile on your face this early in the morning," his partner Bob Snyder said as he leaned against Carter's open office door. While Carter designed Riverside and supervised its construction, Bob saw to it that each unit was rented out and the occupants were happy. He was good at that, while Carter wanted no part of it. And by not having any overlapping duties, their partnership had worked well.

"What can I say? I had a good jog with Fred and even got to hold a very pretty woman in my arms. That ought to be motivation for smiling in anyone's book."

"A pretty woman — hmm — tell me more." Bob strolled into the office and plopped down in one of the upholstered chairs facing Carter's wide glass-topped desk. Dressed in his usual business suit, Bob managed to keep his tie on all day without strangling, instead of just wearing it when he had appointments — a fact about which Carter often marveled.

"Well, let me see if I can remember," he said staring out the side window. "She had strawberry blond hair that glowed red in the bright morning sun, a trim figure that made the comfortable-looking, old sweat-shirt and sweatpants that she wore look great, a cute little nose, and two big, beautiful bluish-gray eyes that crinkled at the corners when she smiled."

Slapping his hand on the arm of the chair, Bob laughed. "Yeah, I'd say you remember very well. But tell me, why don't I know anything of this beauty if you've held her in your arms already this morning?"

Carter barked a laugh. "I actually know very little about her. I literally ran into her this morning while I was out jogging." Remembering holding her close, he shook his head slowly and swung back around in his chair to face Bob. "I've never seen her before, but I'm going jogging at the same time tomorrow to see if I can replay the encounter. And next time I won't let her go so easily — at least not without getting her name and number."

"Sounds like a plan, but good luck having that happen twice in a row." He straightened in his seat. "Say, when do you think the drawings for the next phase of Riverside will be ready to show off, so we can get a start on the backing?" Bob asked in an abrupt change of subject.

"Get right back to business, huh?" Carter grinned. "Don't worry. I'll have them ready by November first, as promised. Right now, I'm waiting on the city to give me elevations for the dikes they're putting in south of us. I want to make sure we will stay high and dry even in a hundred-year flood."

With a slap of his hands on his thighs, his partner rose. A large man, his white shirt separated slightly between the buttons and his belt dug into his generous waistline — evidence that he preferred fine dining to exercise. "Okay, I'd better get back to my office. I sent Ted out with our first eviction notice. It's too bad, though, because they always pay their rent on time."

"And there's a problem with that?" Carter asked with a frown.

"When they lie on their lease about the kind of store they plan to open, and the other store owners complain about them, there is. But we have a waiting list to get in, so it's not a problem for us — one out and another one in." He shrugged. "It's a simple issue, and this is the quickest way to deal with it. See you later," Bob said with a wave of his hand as he left the office.

Thankful that sort of problem didn't fall under his jurisdiction in the company, Carter flicked on the lamp over his slanted drawing table against the wall beside his desk, and went back to checking the dimen-

27

sions of the steps for Riverside Two. Extending for several more blocks along the water, the new section included more than just shops and restaurants. He'd designed luxury condominiums on the highest elevation at the far end, with a common area that included a park, tennis courts, and a swimming pool for tenant use.

The best part was that he'd already earmarked one of the apartments, with a view similar to that from his office, for Fred and himself. He suddenly realized he would have to make certain that they didn't exclude pets from the building. He knew Bob wasn't all that fond of dogs, but Carter found their adoring companionship very gratifying. In the time he'd had Fred, Carter had ignored Bob's complaints about a dog in the office. He's always seen to it that Fred was on his best behavior and figured that Bob couldn't object to that.

After stopping that morning for the visit to the veterinarian, who volunteered her time and skills to care for rescued puppies, Terri loaded them back into her huge padded basket so she could carry them all at once into the shop. The vet had viewed their chances of a healthy future with cautious optimism, and that was good news to Terri.

Cleaned up and fed, they looked a lot better than they had the night before.

"Denied good nutrition early in life, they could suffer in ways that won't be discovered for some time," the vet had said. "We can just hope for the best."

In the meantime, Terri was determined to keep them clean and fed to give them the best chance she could. She waited patiently as the vet examined each one and gave them some of the shots and procedures they should have had by this age. Terri had brought in rescued puppies often enough to know that she would stretch out the treatments so as not to overload the little things in their weakened condition.

Finally, the little balls of fur huddling in their cage in the back of her car, she headed for her shop. Not having had the time that morning to call the volunteers to come in and help, she fed the puppies first thing after introducing them to Sue Harding, a sales assistant, and Tom Waters, the dog-treat baker. From then on, Terri was so busy with customers that she didn't even get her second cup of coffee that morning.

With Sue's help, the calls finally went out to the volunteers for help. They all were eager to feed the formula to the new puppies, or just to gently play with them. Until these little guys were stronger, however, Terri had to put off the playing part. Just holding them to keep them warm and gently petting them was fine. The puppies would have to build up stamina to do more than that.

Caring for them would be much easier when they could begin eating solid food, but for now they each had to be bottle-fed. Soon it would be time for her and the animal shelter to work together to find them permanent homes. She wouldn't entertain any conjecture that the end result would be any different. She always hoped for the best, but she remembered every one of the few puppies that she had lost over the years. Losing even one of them had been too many in her book.

Finally slipping into the back room to get some coffee, she heard the bell on the door ring yet again. She'd barely stirred in a little sugar and taken the first hot sip when her assistant Sue stuck her head into her office and told her she had company. That was their agreed on signal when someone other than a customer had come into the shop and wanted to see Terri. Frowning, she rose and followed Sue out to the front.

"Ms. Terri Bookman?" a young, thin man asked. He looked to be in his twenties and dressed in dark slacks and a shirt and tie plus a sports coat that could use a good pressing.

Terri nodded and slipped her hands into her pants' pockets when he didn't move to shake her hand. She wasn't used to men not even offering to shake hands upon meeting her. "What can I do for you?"

Opening his briefcase, he pulled out some folded papers and handed them to her. "I'm Ted Ryan from M&S Development."

Terri smiled, half expecting him to congratulate her on the sweeping success of her shop. Her smile disappeared instantly when he added, "I'm here to give you this eviction notice."

His words hit her like a blow to the midsection. "You're serving me with an eviction notice?" Feeling her eyes go wide with surprise, she took the papers and unfolded them as she struggled for each breath she took. Her heart raced as she read her name and the name of her shop, K-Nine Treats, right at the top. "But I don't understand. This must be a mistake. I've paid every month's rent and right on time."

"Yes, but you fraudulently represented your shop on the lease agreement. Other owners have complained about all the dogs on the walkway, so we have no choice. You'll

31

see when you read it, the notice gives you thirty days to vacate these premises," he announced coldly.

"But you can't do that. What's this about? I didn't lie about anything. I have a copy of what I filled out, and it's all there. And it's all the truth."

"No, you represented your shop as a bakery. We expected people to buy treats here that many of them would eat while availing themselves of the wrought iron tables and chairs set by the waterfront — weather permitting, of course. From there they could see the other shops and hopefully visit them too."

"But I don't understand. . . ."

"We thought you would be an asset and bring customers in to other shops. Instead, the treats you bake here aren't fit for humans, and the other shops complain nearly daily of your dogs."

"Why would they complain about my dogs? I keep them in my shop, and they never get out on the walkway. I go out the back door in the kitchen when I walk them. And I always pick up after them. I've got the plastic bag dispenser right there outside the door for the public to use too. Why would other owners complain about that?"

"Well, they're not upset about your dogs

per se, but about the many dogs all your customers bring with them. Those dogs are nuisances."

"Look, you can't be serious about this. K-Nine Treats is exactly what the lease states. We bake fresh treats every day for dogs. We have customers in nearly a dozen states already that we ship to, and we've only been in business for six months."

"Then you can take your business to one of those states, because you're not staying here," he said nastily. "We wanted a specialty bakery and that's obviously not what you are."

Suddenly, Terri grinned. "The rental agent didn't realize the meaning of the name K-Nine, or at least he didn't pay attention, did he? He signed me up thinking we baked for people, not for their dogs."

The pained look on Ted's face told her that she had guessed correctly, and that was enough to make her laugh. That only upset the man more.

"K-Nine, K-Two, K-Three, it doesn't matter to him."

"I take it he doesn't like dogs," she put in.

"Look, within thirty days, we'll have signs up to restrict dogs to the grassy area by the water, far from the walkway where they bother people."

"No, *you* look," she countered, too tired to keep her anger in check. "Everything in my lease is the truth. Your boss has no grounds for eviction, and I'm not moving."

"No, Ms. Bookman, the eviction stands. If you wish to take it up with my boss, Mr. Robert Snyder at M&S Development, that's up to you. All I'm here for today is to deliver that," he said, pointing to the eviction notice that hung from her hand. "Have a nice day."

With a fake smile that would have had more feeling if drawn on his face with a colored felt-tip marker, he turned on the ball of his foot and marched out the front door. Terri watched him leave, her arms dropping to her sides as numbness settled into her limbs. Had the perfect world she had worked so hard to create just tumbled down around her?

"They can't do that," a customer, who had heard the whole exchange, said. "I just found you. I can't lose you now."

"Why would they close a shop that paid its rent and is as popular as yours?" another shopper, who was cuddling one of the puppies, asked.

Embarrassed at having her problems made so public, Terri didn't feel up to any second-guessing. Shaking her head, she smiled at the ladies but felt her lower lip quiver. "I don't know," she managed. "And thank you for your concern."

"You're not going to let them get away with that, are you?" Sue asked.

"No, I sure hope not," Terri said, taking a deep breath. "I guess I'll start by seeing Bob Snyder, the rental agent who apparently doesn't like dogs. I have a copy of all the lease papers, and I'll just prove to him that they describe the store exactly as it is."

"Anyone could tell what it was by the name," a customer put in.

Terri shrugged, but Sue snorted a laugh. "They read 'treat bakery' and signed on the dotted line — I mean, like, duh!"

"Sue, I'm going to call about getting that appointment. You can help these ladies to be sure the puppies are safely back in their spot when they're done, can't you?" Terri said in reference to the two customers already there and the third who had just come in and headed right for the puppy pen.

"Oh, and I want to buy that adorable sweater for Petey too. It gets cooler every day now that fall is here," the first customer added. "I hate to see him shiver."

"Sure," Sue said. "I'll be happy to help you with that."

As Sue turned to show the way to the sweaters, Terri walked into her office. The

35

boys, who accompanied her to work each day and kept her company as she worked on the books, greeted her excitedly. Their affectionate kisses went a long way toward improving her mood.

Sitting in her desk chair with a sigh, she unlocked the file cabinet beside her desk and reread her lease agreement. Yes, it was all there. She had even itemized many of the accessories she would carry.

But now, as she read the list that included sweaters, raincoats, boots, hats, and vests, she realized that if one had no imagination, they all might refer to human clothing as well as to the doggy versions she carried. And other than the name of the shop, the word dog was not on the paper — in any language. And she'd been so sure that her lawyer had made it all so clear.

But what people-bakery would sell clothes? That idea was crazy.

What a mess it all was. And just when things had been going so well.

Not wanting to put off solving the problem any longer, she reached for her telephone and the file of numbers beside it. Several minutes later, she had an appointment the following afternoon with the rental agent at M&S Development Company.

She needed to be able to solve this to

remain where she was — where business was so good. And she would. Going back to her former location downtown was impossible. She wouldn't go through that again with a landlord she couldn't trust.

CHAPTER TWO

"Looks like my luck is holding," Carter said in a low voice to Fred the next morning when he saw the pretty woman with the two little dogs jogging toward him from the opposite direction on the path. Here was his chance to strike up a conversation, and this time he would get her name, he silently vowed.

The way she jogged in tiny steps so her dogs could keep on leading the way was cute. He reached her in no time at full speed and grinned as Fred turned to greet her dogs that were barking with excitement. This time she shortened the leashes and kept her dogs in front of her.

Reversing his direction to match hers by jogging in place until she was even with him on the path, he adapted to her speed and ran alongside of her. Her dogs pranced happily and settled into jogging beside Fred.

"Our dogs act like old friends," he said,

adjusting Fred's leash so he could run next to her dogs. With a grin, he added, "I think the least we can do is introduce ourselves since our dogs get along so well."

She laughed and he liked the way her mirth made her eyes sparkle. "I've got to give you credit. I've never heard that line before."

"I'm Carter Morris and this is Fred," he said, gesturing toward his Lab.

"Hi. I'm Terri Bookman and the boys are Day and Night."

Carter felt his grin broadening. "Do I need to guess which is Day and which is Night?"

She laughed. "No, the white one is actually Day. Since I didn't name them, I'll be thankful for what I got."

"Have you had them long?"

"Long enough to do more with their training, but I'm always so busy at work that I haven't had the time to be consistent with them. I do know that's the key in training dogs."

"Yeah, it is. And actually I like working with Fred 'cause it gives me a time I can forget all about work."

She looked at him quizzically. "Your life must not be happy if you have a job you dislike enough to want to escape from it."

"Oh, no, I love my work. I didn't mean that. I just need to let it go and reduce the stress sometimes. Fred helps a lot with that, and then I can return to work with fresh ideas."

"What do you do?"

"I'm an architect. And don't get me wrong, I really do love the work. I've wanted to be an architect since I was this high," he said, holding his hand out in front of him with the palm down at his waist level. "I used to draw building plans even back then."

"Life is so much more pleasant doing what you like to do," she said as she slowed her pace until she stopped. "Well, this is where I leave you. It was nice meeting you, Carter. Maybe we'll see you jogging at the same time again."

Carter stopped at her side and Fred promptly sat beside him in the heel position. "Let's not leave it to chance. Can we have lunch?" He named a popular restaurant just a couple of blocks from Riverside. She met his gaze, and he could tell she was sizing him up and deciding whether she should meet him or not. "I know you don't know anything about me, but it's a big restaurant with lots of people around," he said. "And I promise I'll be on my best behavior," he added with a wink.

"Anyone who has a dog as well behaved as Fred has got to be someone I could trust. Sure, I'll meet you there for lunch. I have an appointment not far from there at two."

"Shall we meet at twelve-thirty, then? Will that give you enough time?"

"Sure, I don't eat that much," she replied with a laugh.

Unable to resist, his gaze slid over the blue exercise suit she wore. The top was zipped most of the way, and he couldn't read what her tee shirt said, but he could tell she filled it nicely. It was much newer than yesterday's outfit, and he wondered for a moment if she had worn it in case they met again. The thought made him smile more broadly. "See you there," he said.

She nodded and took off. Watching as she ran toward a silver SUV parked on the street, he felt pleased with himself. Opening the back door, she lifted her dogs up and in. They went right into their carriers, and she shut the doors before closing the hatch.

Realizing he wanted to watch her longer made him turn back onto the path and begin jogging again. "Come on, Fred. I'd better get to work if I'm going to take a long lunch. I may own half the place, but I still have to put in a day's work."

■ ■ ■ ■

Terri's morning flew by as she looked forward to the lunch with Carter. After getting out of her best jogging suit that she'd been so glad she'd worn that morning, she took her shower.

The puppies were anxious to get their bottles before she loaded them up in the sturdy carrier. The fact that they were hungry and ate the full amount she'd prepared was a good sign. Once tucked into their blanket, they promptly fell asleep as usual.

Terri took the opportunity to get dressed in her deep navy pantsuit. She softened the nearly black color with a pale blue blouse. She would wear no K-Nine tee shirt for work today, not with the lunch and appointment with her landlord right after it. She also spent a few extra minutes on her makeup and hair. When she realized what she was doing, she dropped her powder brush on the bath vanity and laughed at herself in the mirror.

"He's only a guy you just met who seems nice and asked you to lunch," she said to her reflection.

"I know. I know," she replied to herself.

"But he's so good looking," she added with another laugh as she switched off the light and left the room.

Grabbing her purse, she returned to the hall where she'd left the carrier. The rescued puppies looked so cute with their tummies getting more rounded each day, the way they should be at this age. Once she got them and the boys to the car, she loaded them in the back where they would be safe and drove to the shop.

Inhaling the fresh fall air, she paused while the boys relieved themselves on the little lawn by the parking lot. She entered the store by the back door, walking into the kitchen where Tom was already at work.

"Morning, Terri," he called from the ovens where he was taking out trays of freshly baked treats. His day started an hour before the shop opened, which gave him plenty of time to start the day off right with a fresh batch of the bone-shaped treats from the dough he'd mixed and refrigerated the night before.

Before Sue showed up just before the shop opened, Terri had her paperwork and her copy of the lease packed into her slim leather briefcase sitting on her desk chair ready for her departure at noon. Even going over the important details, her memory of that morning distracted her and served up flashes of Carter's handsome face and his engaging smile. Even though she knew little about him, his effect on her was a feeling of calm because he seemed so solid and trustworthy. It was nice to meet a man she felt could be trusted.

Filling in Sue about her schedule and telling her about the lunch with Carter, she tried to keep the mention casual. Sue knew she didn't date much with all her time devoted to the shop. She didn't want Sue to get the wrong idea about the date being more than it really was — a first chance to get acquainted.

As she touched up her lipstick, Terri thought of the rude young man who had stopped in the day before. Terri still didn't understand getting the eviction notice that he'd handed her. There had to have been a mistake on M&S's part. She hadn't told any falsehoods in the deal, so when the time came to leave for lunch, she was confident that her meeting at M&S that afternoon would work out just fine.

Checking in the mirror on the back of her office closet door one last time, she fluffed her short hair and straightened the collar on her suit jacket. She rarely wore nice clothes to the shop, since she was constantly sitting on the floor with all the puppies. Whatever she wore seemed to attract a few dog hairs, which now she brushed off.

"You're sure you don't want me to come to lunch with you?" Sue asked with a smile, sticking her head into Terri's office.

"Oh, no you don't. You're a happily married woman and besides, three's a crowd at this lunch." She chuckled. "You know, after being all work and no play for a couple of years, I miss going out for lunch. I'm not blowing this chance at having a good time."

"He must be a hunk if you want him all to yourself."

Terri tipped her head and thought for a minute. "Yeah, maybe you're right," she said, blowing her casual act all to pieces.

"I knew it," Sue replied with a laugh. "Well, have fun and don't worry about us here. We have a steady stream of regulars coming in to help with the puppies, and the boys love it here when you're gone."

"They should with all the treats that Tom smuggles to them."

"Uh-oh, he thinks you never notice, but remember, they're good for them too," Sue countered as she followed Terri across the shop to the entrance.

"I'm not complaining. It's another excuse to keep jogging in the morning. See you after my appointment at M&S. I'm not sure how late I'll be."

"That's fine. Just come back whenever."

Terri held the door for a customer entering the store, and then walked out with a wave over her shoulder. When she walked into the restaurant twenty minutes later, she saw Carter sitting at a table in the corner watching for her, and she smiled. He rose and extended his left hand. She slipped her right into it and the gentle squeeze she received was warm and sent delightful tingles farther up her arm. After waiting for her to sit down, he sat opposite her at the small round table.

"I'm glad you came. I wasn't sure you would," he admitted.

Taking a moment, she smiled as she rested her briefcase and purse against the front leg of her chair. Not wanting anything to happen to her copy of the lease papers, she wanted the case where she could keep a close watch on it.

"I'm glad I came too. I . . . ," she said and then paused. She had started to say that she wanted to see him again. Instead, she said, "I thought lunch with a new friend would be nice in the middle of my hectic day."

"Good," he said settling back in his chair.

Slipping her napkin onto her lap, she

picked up her menu and scanned it. "I haven't eaten here before. Do you recommend anything?"

"If I eat too much I fall asleep at my drafting table, so I generally pick one of the seafood salads. I like their fresh homemade dressings."

The waiter approached the table and asked if they were ready to order. Carter nodded after Terri said she was ready. He waited while she took his advice and ordered a mixed-greens salad with shrimp and a citrus dressing. When the waiter asked if she wanted anything to drink besides ice water, she added a glass of iced tea to her order. He asked for a tuna steak salad with the tuna done medium and a glass of tea as well. As the waiter left, they relaxed back into their seats.

"So what is making your day so hectic? The boys giving you trouble?"

"No, but I acquired three tiny puppies that are taking a lot of my time. They have to be bottle-fed every few hours and gently cuddled a lot as they build up their strength."

"You acquired them?"

She nodded. "I help out the animal shelter when they have puppies that need special care for one reason or another. They sometimes have more than they can handle."

"Were these orphaned?"

"Yes and no — no one had cared for them, which is why they were rescued. Now they don't quite know what to make of life without a mother. She didn't make it. They like getting food and water on a regular basis though. That's a big change for them."

He shook his head. "It sounds admirable, but you've got a handful of work."

She laughed and nodded. "They were rescued from a home that had so many dogs that the Animal Rescue officers are still picking them up as they come home to the house after wandering around on their own."

"You're not taking more now."

"No, I just take puppies when the animal shelter has too many. They really need a bigger facility for a growing town this size. But even now, they don't have the staff to handle puppies that aren't weaned yet. It means a lot of bottle feedings."

"I see. You help by taking the overflow home with you?"

"I do when I can. Sam calls me when they need help. He's the Animal Rescue officer in charge. In this case, they took in all the older dogs, but I got the babies 'cause their mother couldn't feed them. They took her straight to the vet, but the rescue came too late for her."

Terri blinked away the tears that burned at the back of her eyes. Her puppies would have a mother if the owner hadn't over-bred and underfed her.

"I'm sorry."

Their conversation paused as the waiter placed their iced teas on the table.

"What happens to them all when you go to work?" Carter asked after taking a sip. "And I'm assuming you do work during the days."

She laughed. "Yes, I work at a shop at Riverside. I can take the dogs to work with me because I have a group of regulars who come in to help feed and cuddle them, or to do whatever needs to be done. That way I don't have to do it all."

"That must be an unusual business to allow that to go on during working hours."

"Yeah, you could say that," she said with a little laugh.

The waiter brought a basket of rolls and a dish of softened butter in the shape of a daisy. Terri decided against the extra carbs and motioned Carter to them. He took one with a little butter and set it on his bread dish.

During this pause in their conversation,

Terri had decided that until she knew Carter better — if she came to know Carter better — she wouldn't share any specifics about her owning the shop. She didn't like flaunting that information. If he only knew she worked there for now, that was enough.

"The puppies are adorable. They do keep me busy, but I'm happy that, unlike their mother, it looks like they'll all make it."

"I think the world needs more people like you who would donate so much of their time and effort. On behalf of all the dogs you help, I thank you." Smiling broadly, he tipped his head toward her in a tribute.

His compliment flowed over her and felt good. "Thanks."

"It can't be easy feeding puppies every few hours. That would be like having newborn babies to feed. Or do you have help for the feedings at home?"

Meeting his gaze, she wondered if he were curious about her sleep schedule or her living arrangements. "No, I live alone," she said in a softer voice. She cleared her throat and looked down at her napkin under the guise of straightening it on her lap. "And I could have used some help with three puppies to clean up and feed when I picked them up the other night," she added in a firmer voice. She shrugged. "I guess I got

50

about as many hours of sleep as I have puppies. If I yawn during lunch, I hope you'll
understand."

Smiling, he said, "Why not call me the
next time you go to help rescue any? I'll
lend a hand if I can."

Seeing no guile or mockery in his face,
she nodded. "Thanks. And wouldn't you be
surprised if I did?"

"No, I mean it. Is that how you acquired
the boys? Night and Day — did you rescue
them too?"

"Oh, you remembered their names," she
remarked, thinking that was very clever of
him after hearing them only once. "Well,
it's sort of that way. Sam called me about
them, yes, but they weren't rescued from an
abusive situation. An elderly woman in town
owned them but couldn't afford to keep
them. The fact is that with the little money
she had, she took better care of them than
she did of herself."

He frowned but didn't interrupt.

"When her daughter came into town for
her regular visit, she found her mother
nearly starved and the boys fat and happy,
wanting to go out and play. She's the one
who called Sam. She took her mother home
with her instead of leaving her here to live
alone too. She couldn't take the dogs, so

51

Sam did."

The waiter returned to their table and set their salad plates before them. When they said there was nothing else that they needed, he returned to his other duties.

"But they weren't puppies. Sam couldn't find a home somewhere else for them?"

She shook her head as she chewed and swallowed her first bite of salad. "Once I saw them, I knew I had to have them. Now I couldn't part with them. They're so cute and loveable, and they're great company."

"You're not going to try to keep the three puppies too, are you?" he asked as he cut a slice of tuna on top of his salad.

"No, I may be a dreamer, but I'm a practical dreamer." She frowned. "Or is that an oxymoron?" She laughed. "I do know when to draw the line."

After another bite of salad, she asked, "How long have you had Fred?"

"He's been with me for a couple of years. I know there are those who think it's bad to leave him home in my apartment some days, but I make sure he gets exercise and is walked when he needs to be outside. If I get tied up on the days he's at home, I send my assistant over to walk him. They get along great, and if you asked me, I think my assistant is happy to leave the office for a while. In fact, now that I think of it, when Fred's at the office with me, everyone gets along with Fred — except my partner, but he just doesn't like dogs."

"Fred's a sweetie. I don't see how someone could help but like him."

They chatted on about breeds and temperaments as they finished their lunches.

"That was a yummy salad. You were right about the dressing — light and delicious," Terri said as she laid her fork and knife together on her plate.

"You up for dessert?" he asked, doing the same.

"No, thanks. I couldn't eat another thing." She glanced at her watch. "I have to leave soon anyway. My appointment is over at M&S Development, so it's not far."

He frowned and shifted in his seat. "Is it about the shop where you work?"

Terri met his gaze and decided suddenly she could tell him. "Actually, ah . . . I own the business where I work, and yes, it's about that."

He grinned. "No wonder you can take dogs to work if you own it," he put in.

"Rank does have its privileges," she said with a grin. "I have a fenced run that the boys can follow out from my office into the shop along one wall to see the customers. I

53

don't let them run free because I worry that might bother some customers." She laughed. "Who am I kidding? I don't let them loose because they would discover all the dog treats I sell and help themselves." She wiped the corners of her mouth on her napkin. "As you know, discipline isn't their strong suit and they do love to eat."

"They seem very excitable."

"Nice way of putting it, but we're working on calming down and not having them bark their heads off at other dogs." She set her napkin on the table beside her plate. "This has been fun, but I guess I should go. I don't want to be late for my meeting."

Taking out her wallet, she was about to leave the amount for her lunch when he laid his hand over hers.

"I asked you to lunch, and the lunch is on me."

"You don't have to . . . ," she began to reply.

"I know, but I want to," he responded quietly.

"Thank you." Returning her wallet to her purse, she picked up her briefcase and rested them on her thighs for a few moments. "I'm glad you suggested lunch."

"Me too, and I have to guess that dinner together might be fun too."

Her heartbeat increased at hearing he wanted to see her again. She laughed lightly. "That could be."

"May I call you?"

Nodding, she said, "I'd like that. I'm in the book."

Rising with her purse and briefcase, she thanked him again and exited the restaurant. On the sidewalk outside, she looked back in, through the windows, at their table. Carter was still there watching her. Caught getting another look at him, she smiled and walked on.

Carter waited until she disappeared from sight before he signaled the waiter and got their bill. He paid it quickly with his credit card and left. What lousy luck. Out of all the women he could be attracted to, he had to pick the owner of one of the shops in his own development. He'd always resisted becoming involved with any of their rental clients because of the problems it might lead to. At least he hadn't told her where he worked. If she were having problems, it wouldn't be good for her to ask him to help.

But when he thought about it, Terri would be dealing with Bob and not him. If her appointment at M&S had been because of a problem with the building, he would learn about it in order to solve it. Other than that, there was no way he would even know about her appointment or the reason for it. Because no one mentioned her coming to the office to him, he had to assume it had nothing to do with him. That meant there was no reason he couldn't keep seeing her, he concluded. She would eventually learn of his half-ownership of M&S, but it wouldn't be any different from telling her the name of any other company for which he worked.

Besides, how much of a problem could a pretty woman who spent her nights taking care of rescued puppies be? No, he couldn't see dating her as a problem.

Rubbing the back of his neck where something made him feel a bit itchy, he tried to think if he'd heard anything at the office about her appointment. Her name wasn't all that unusual, but he would have remembered it if Bob had mentioned it. No, it was something other than her name that nagged at him, but he couldn't remember what it was about.

During lunch, he'd wanted to stop talking about M&S, so he hadn't asked why she had an appointment there. Tenant relations was his partner's domain. Often not paying attention to the shop-owner specifics, Carter left the day-to-day running of the development up to his partner Bob and his eager young staff. Frankly, he was glad those duties didn't come under his jurisdiction. He designed the shops and saw that they were built right. That's all he wanted to do.

Unable to remember what about Terri or her shop had rung a bell in his memory, he headed for the parking lot where he quickly found his pickup truck. He'd stashed his drawings and equipment in the cab before lunch. Pulling out into traffic, he headed for the new site farther down the river where Riverside Two would soon begin to take shape.

Chapter Three

"Ms. Bookman, you may go in now," the receptionist told Terri after keeping her waiting nearly fifteen minutes beyond the appointed time for her to talk with the M&S rental agent.

Entering the plush office, she tried to ignore the huge polished cherry wood desk, the table at one end of the room with eight upholstered chairs around it, and the sideboard with the pitcher of ice water and four glasses on an inlaid-wood tray. Instead of making her feel comfortable, such lavish surroundings made her feel just the opposite. This wasn't Donald Trump's office, after all. No, this was the company that was trying to kick her out when she hadn't done anything wrong. Her backbone stiffened with renewed resolve.

The man behind the desk, Bob Snyder, according to what was carved in his brass-and-cherry nameplate, rose and stepped around the desk toward her. "Ms. Bookman, how are you?" he asked with a broad smile as he raised his hand to shake hers. To look at the man, one would never think that he held her livelihood on the edge of a sword that could easily cut it into pieces.

His handshake involved just grasping her bent fingers and lasted only seconds — more like a light squeeze than a shake. It felt insincere and dismissive to her and added one more notch to her ire.

"I'd be better if I could understand why you are trying to evict me when I've never missed paying my rent on time."

"Well now, let's take a look at our agreement, shall we? After we go through it, I'm sure you'll understand that what you wrote was misleading to say the least. With all the complaints from the other shop owners at Riverside, we just cannot have you continue in business there." He waved his hand toward one of the two upholstered chairs facing his desk and sat back down in his own chair behind the desk without waiting for her to seat herself.

Seated where he had pointed, Terri opened her briefcase and extracted her copy of the lease agreement. For the next twenty minutes, they discussed each line that described K-Nine Treats. Bob had interpreted them to mean a bakery specializing in sweet treats. Terri insisted that the name K-Nine clearly spelled out the fact that the treats and accessories sold there were for dogs. "Why would the kind of bakery you thought it was sell clothes or leashes?" she persisted.

He ignored her objections and the question as if she hadn't spoken at all. "We rented to you because we thought a specialty bakery would be wonderful at Riverside. I'm sorry you didn't open the kind of store that we were led to expect. And despite your objections, I cannot see my way clear to stop the eviction notice. We gave you thirty days, which is all that is required of us, but to show you that we appreciate your paying your rent on time and your cooperation, I'll give you another thirty days."

"I can have thirty more?"

"Yes, but you will have to be out by November fifteenth. I have another shop that will move in then, and I know they'll want to gear up immediately for the Christmas buying season."

He looked down at his desk in a dismissive gesture, but then jerked his head up. "Oh, and we're going ahead with the new rule that prohibits dogs from the walkway in front of the shops. Besides being too much of a danger to our shoppers, they're a nuisance and very messy too. People don't always pick up after them like they should."

That did it. Terri felt her temperature peak.

"I'm sorry too, Mr. Snyder," she said as she slipped her lease back into her briefcase and rose. "I'm sorry you won't live up to your side of the agreement, as it is written very clearly to describe exactly the kind of shop I opened. And I want you to know that I intend to fight this eviction. My lawyer will be in contact with you. I know he'll want a list of all the other owners who have complained about my shop and a copy of their complaints, so you'll want to have them on hand."

She strode to the door and stopped with her hand on the knob to look back at him. He had not even risen from his seat and just stared at her as if she had two heads. "Have a good day, Mr. Snyder."

With that Terri exited his office and the building. Her heart was pounding rapidly, and her hands felt cold and clammy. She hated confrontations like the one she'd just had, but she wasn't about to let that man tromp all over her dream that had just begun to come true. Her first landlord had acted like such a jerk that she'd moved out of his building. But now this one wanted to get rid of her on false pretenses. Well, nobody said owning her own business would be easy.

Walking briskly back to her car, she climbed in behind the wheel, plopped her case on the passenger seat, and leaned back against the headrest for a few minutes to give herself time to calm down so she could drive safely.

How could they even try to do this to her? All the horrid things he said about her misleading them about the kind of shop she was opening were untrue. She had to fight.

And why would they restrict the wide walk in front of the shops to people only? He'd said they were going to keep out all dogs. He thought they were too much of a danger to other customers? Bah, humbug! — the dogs that came into her shop with customers weren't a danger to anyone. The small ones were mostly in carriers and the large dogs were sweet and docile. Would her customers want to come buy treats and accessories if they couldn't bring in their dogs for treat-tastings and fittings?

If Bob Snyder had his way, they couldn't come in at all. And if dogs were outlawed from the walk in front of the shops, her customers with their dogs couldn't get to her front entrance. That would mean the end of her business even without the eviction notice.

After working so long and hard to build a successful company, she had to keep the shop open. It was a wonderful location and she just plain didn't want to move.

And she wasn't going to. There had to be a way to keep the shop where it was. But the only option she saw to keep the shop there was to hire a lawyer to fight the eviction.

Shaking her head, she started her car and drove back to K-Nine Treats. What would it cost to hire a lawyer to defend her? Where would she get the money to pay for her defense? The shop was doing well now, but she still had the initial loan for fixtures and stock that she was paying off. She wasn't even certain the bank would loan her more until that was paid off.

And what if she paid for the lawyer and somehow they lost anyway? With little in savings for a rainy day, she could end up in a deep financial hole from which she would never emerge.

Pressing her fingers against her temple didn't stop the throbbing pain that was building there, nor did walking into her shop and seeing buying customers lined up at the register. Dropping her case and purse in her office, she hung her suit jacket on her office chair and went to help Sue. The line didn't disappear until closing time that evening, but it still didn't seem to lighten her mood.

"Another great day," Sue said as she cashed out the register drawer once the doors were locked. This was Sue's first job after raising three children to high school age. With college expenses looming large and near, she had joined the work force to add to the family's savings.

Tom came out from the kitchen, his baker's apron tossed over his shoulder. Somewhere in his late fifties, he had been a chef in his own small diner near the highway. Called the Watering Hole, it had been a popular gathering place where everyone knew Tom Waters and his wife. However, when his wife died just over a year ago, he'd decided to sell the diner and look for work somewhere else. He needed to work in a kitchen that wasn't filled with memories of her, he'd told Terri. She felt lucky to have him working for her because she knew he wasn't making as much money as he had at his own place.

"Everything's cleaned up and put away," he announced. "You had so many customers today that I made dough for ten percent more bone-shaped treats for tomorrow. That will help build the stock on the shelves back up."

"Good," Terri said to encourage him to make such decisions without her input.

"How'd the meeting go today?" he asked hesitantly. "We . . . well, Sue and me were wondering if we'd have jobs for more than thirty days."

Terri leaned back against the counter. "I sure hope so, Tom, but right now I can't promise anything except thirty more days beyond that. You guys certainly deserve to know all that happened today, but I didn't want to discuss it in front of the customers."

"So what did they tell you at M&S?" Sue asked.

Explaining the whole conversation including the thirty-day extension, Terri didn't leave any details out. "I don't know how to fight it other than to hire a lawyer to defend me. And I just know that will cost a lot." She sighed heavily under the weight of her problems.

"Just talking to a lawyer to see what he recommends might not cost a lot," Sue suggested with a shrug. "I know one who helped a friend of mine when she couldn't get her security deposit back from her landlord after she moved out. He simply had to go and tell the landlord that he was prepared to fight for the return of every cent, and the landlord gave him a check to avoid legal action. It only cost her an hour of his time. Maybe M&S would do the same if the lawyer showed up there."

Terri laughed. "I don't think it'll be that easy. The owners of M&S don't have any money problems. If you sold everything in the M&S rental guy's office you could pay for a lawyer for a month several times over. They probably have one on retainer and won't buckle, but I don't see that I have a choice at this point."

"Why don't you let me talk to the lawyer I know?" Sue offered. "His name is Blake Roberts, and he lives down the block from us. I see him mowing his lawn every Saturday so I could talk to him then. Or, if you want, I can call him tonight."

"Why not ask him Saturday? That's only two days away, and I really should contact the lawyer who helped me draw up the lease papers first." She glanced at her watch. "I can't reach him until tomorrow during business hours. If he can help me, I'll tell you tomorrow because that would mean I won't need your neighbor."

"Great. And if I don't hear from you, I'll

talk to Blake on Saturday."

Tom headed for the door. Sue took her purse out of a drawer beneath the cash register and followed him. Slipping her arms into her coat, she called back over her shoulder, "See you in the morning. Oh, and the volunteers just fed the puppies an hour ago, in case you were too busy to notice the schedule. Those little guys sure are growing."

"That's good news, and it's thanks to their getting some nutritious food. Good night and thanks," Terri said, following them to the door.

A cold breeze portending even colder weather blew in before she could get the door closed after them and locked again. Fall was here and winter wasn't far behind. She walked over to the small kiddie swimming pool lined with blankets over newspapers that she kept in the shop for the puppies. Awake now, they yipped with excitement as she approached, the whole rear ends of their bodies moving from side to side as they wagged their tails.

"You sure do have more energy than when I got you. Ready to go home, kids?"

Petting each one in turn, she had to smile. No matter how down she felt, playing with a dog always cheered her up. Her own dogs acted jealous of the attention she paid to the puppies, so she released them from their run. They danced around her legs as she gave them each a good back scratch and hug.

"Be right back," she promised the puppies as she prepared to leave for the night. "You guys come with me. Come."

Her dogs followed her into her office where she got into her coat and grabbed her purse and the deposit pouch to drop off at the bank on the drive home. Ten minutes later she had all three puppies bundled up in the basket that hung over her arm. Her own dogs were on leashes for the walk to her car.

As she left the building, she glanced at the CLOSED sign that she had hung in the door earlier. There had to be a way to keep this shop from being permanently closed. She just had to find it.

"Terri? It's Sam. Sorry if I woke you, but I have more puppies than I know what to do with here."

"But I've got the three you just gave me last week."

"I know, and if I wasn't desperate, I wouldn't have called. There was a barn fire, Terri. Four babies were carried out of the barn to safety, but when their mother went back in for the last one, she barely made it out."

Terri gasped.

"We rushed her to the vet and they say she'll make it, but she can no longer feed her pups. The owners just need help until they get things here back to as normal as they can get at this point. Then they can take them back. They're good people who had a terrible thing happen to them. We're just still too full from last week. Do you think that, with the help you get at the shop, you could take her litter just for a few days?"

"Oh, of course I'll help. Tell me where you are." She wrote down the address on the pad by her phone. "It'll take me twenty or twenty-five minutes to get dressed and out there."

"We'll be here. We're still arranging for transportation of the large animals that got burned before they escaped the flames. And I have to warn you. These puppies are larger than the tiny little buggers you like so much. They're very agitated right now without their mother, and really a handful. But they were already in the weaning stage, so feeding won't be as big a problem as those little ones. You won't need bottles. Do you have anyone you could call this late to get to help you come get them?"

A vision of Carter flashed through her mind. He had offered to help if she needed it. He'd even insisted that he meant his offer. And it sure sounded like she would need help with this bunch.

"Yeah, I'll call and see."

"Thanks, Terri. See you as soon as you can get here."

Terri hung up the phone and hurried into her bedroom to dress. No longer sleepy, she pulled on her usual rescue costume: old jeans and a sweatshirt. They were comfortable as well as practical, and she didn't care if she got them ripped or soiled. And she could just as easily throw them out as wash them.

As she passed the linen closet, she grabbed a few big towels that she'd bought at the Salvation Army for just such emergencies. In the kitchen, she got out a small plastic cooler and filled it with bottles of water from the bottom shelf of her refrigerator. Everyone at the fire was bound to be thirsty. She filled a gallon jug at the sink with water for the puppies. She already had water dishes in the box in the car.

Then, with everything ready, she turned back to the telephone. Sam had never before suggested that she bring a friend to help, so

70

that had to mean that she really would need someone with her. Her women friends seemed to admire what she did, but not one of them had ever offered to leave their warm, comfortable beds and actually go out to help her. Only one person had ever done that — Carter.

"Call him," she ordered herself out loud. "Put your personal attraction aside and think of the dogs who need you both." She groaned, knowing that she'd already stalled long enough to make it easy for him to say no.

Grabbing the phone book, she found Carter's home number and punched it in before she could change her mind. If he couldn't go with her, she would go alone and manage somehow.

"Morris," he answered in a sleep-roughened voice that made it crystal clear that he was annoyed with the late call.

"Carter? It's Terri Bookman."

"Terri, what's wrong? You don't sound like yourself."

"I'm sorry to call you so late, but did you mean it that you would help if I needed you to go pick up some puppies with me?"

"Are we talking about right now? Tonight?"

"Yeah." He didn't sound interested at this

hour. Her heart sank. "I know it's very late . . ."

"No, I want to go."

"You do? Ah . . . that's great. I see by the phone book where you live, but that's in the opposite direction of the rescue. Could you drive to my apartment and then we'll go from here in my car? It's all set up for the puppies."

"That makes sense — sure."

She gave him the address and described where her car was in the parking lot.

"I just need to throw on some clothes. I'll be there ASAP."

"Thanks, Carter. Oh, and wear clothes that can get ruined without it bothering you. Sometimes they get dirty beyond the point of ever being clean again. That includes your jacket."

"I'll do that. You're certain your parking lot is safe for you to wait in at this hour?"

"I've never known there to be a problem."

"Okay, well, it should take me about fifteen minutes to get there."

"I'll be down there and ready to go."

Terri hung up the phone. Knowing he was willing to help her made her feel good. Smiling, she pulled on her heavy jacket and knit cap and stuffed several latex gloves in her pocket, hoping they would stretch to fit Carter's hands too. She never got a chance to wash up before driving home, and using gloves with the dogs meant they could be pulled off to keep her car steering wheel clean. And then there was the fact that the dogs were often filthy, and touching them before they were cleaned up wasn't a good idea.

Once she'd loaded the towels and water into her car, she ran back up to the apartment for her largest travel crate. That would be safer than expecting larger pups to stay in the cardboard box already in the car. She temporarily moved that to the back seat.

After only a short wait of a minute or two in the parking lot, Carter arrived and jumped into her car for the ride to the burned barn. His hair was tousled and sexy looking. The front was damp, and she wondered if he'd splashed his face with cold water to wake himself up.

"Sorry to call so late and wake you up," she said with a smile. "This fire had just no consideration," she added with faux sternness.

"No problem," he replied with a grin as he fastened his seat belt. "Besides, I've always thought that sleep was overrated."

She laughed lightly at his jest. "Well, anyway, thanks," she said as she started the car and headed for their destination.

"How are you going to manage having more dogs?"

"I'll only have tonight's for a short time. They're from a good home that's disrupted by the fire. Once they get back on an even keel, they'll take the dogs back."

"I understand, but if you need more help, let me know."

"Thanks, Carter," she replied, feeling warmed by his offer.

As they drove in the driveway to the farm, they saw that the barn had burned to the ground. The wooden timbers were still smoldering and producing thick smoke. One fire truck was pumping water onto the timbers from the farm pond built nearby for this eventuality. The flashing lights on the police cars and fire trucks pulsed colorful light onto the rising columns of smoke and the cloudy night sky for a long way off.

Fortunately, the flames had not touched the farmhouse on the opposite side of the farmyard. A middle-aged couple dressed in coats pulled on over their nightwear stood there talking with the fire chief. The husband's hands, held out where they wouldn't touch anything, were both bandaged. Terri could see two children looking out the upstairs windows on the front of the house.

Her heart went out to them all. They had experienced a frightening night, and the big job they would have rebuilding still lay ahead of them.

Spotting Sam's Animal Rescue van, she pulled her car over and parked next to it. The puppies, contained in a large metal cage set on the ground, were barking and jumping back and forth trying to get out. She and Carter approached the van as Sam and another officer headed toward it from the driveway that led out the other end of the farmyard. They had just loaded a horse, whose back was swathed in bandages, into a trailer that drove out as they all watched.

"Is he going to be okay?" Terri asked of the horse.

"Yeah, but he may be bald the rest of his life. Boy, I hate to see animals in pain."

Terri introduced Carter to Sam, and they shook hands.

"I'm glad to see she asked you to help her. She takes on Herculean tasks without a second thought if it means helping a dog. She'll need your help with these lively ones."

Terri felt Carter's gaze on her but didn't turn to meet it. She felt too embarrassed at the praise and quickly got the subject off herself. "None of the puppies got near the flames, did they?" she asked Sam.

He shook his head. "I don't think so, but with little good light out here, I'll have to leave checking them carefully to you, especially the last one carried out. The smoke was pretty bad by then."

"They look like sturdy pups," Carter said.

"These folks raise Labs for potential use as aides to the blind," Sam explained. "They have a great bloodline that makes them devoted companions. Their mother did a great job of getting them out of the barn, and at the same time she alerted the family to the fire."

Pulling off his hard hat as he spoke, he wiped off his forehead and the inside of the hat with his handkerchief and put it back on. "It's good for them that it wasn't any later in the year. Then the dogs might have been in the house and wouldn't have known about the fire until it was too late for the horses in there."

Terri noticed other horses in a corral nearer the house. Obviously still upset, they moved around nervously.

"None of them was injured?"

"No, the farmer got them out by pulling feed bags over their heads and slapping their rumps to get them to run. The one that was burned froze and wouldn't leave until he pulled her out. A clump of burning hay fell on her back." He shook his head. "The farmer's hands are going to hurt for a while too. He brushed the hay off of her and got burned in the process."

"Do they know what started the fire?" Carter asked.

"They're not sure. The fire investigators will be back tomorrow in the light of day to figure it out, though."

"Well, let's get the puppies loaded." She turned to Carter and smiled as she handed him a pair of the gloves to keep his hands clean. "I hope these fit." Looking at the agitated pups, she added, "I'm really glad you came with me. These guys do look like more than a handful." When she turned back to Carter, Terri noticed a twinkle in his eye and a smoldering spark in his smile that clearly communicated his attraction to her — and somehow she knew, then and there, that they would share more smiles in the future.

Chapter Four

After Sam opened the cage behind his truck, each of them picked up a puppy. Exuberant little guys, they licked at their human helpers' faces and wiggled in their arms, showing how happy they were to be held.

"It's okay, little fellow. You're safe now," Terri assured the one she held. When those dogs were deposited in the travel crate, they went back for the last ones.

"These have been well cared for and have all their shots," Sam told her. "So there are no worries there."

"The other puppies have started theirs, but I'll keep them separate as usual. The others are way too little to be safe with these playful big guys, anyway."

"Right," Sam agreed. "How are the little ones doing?"

"I think they'll all make it," Terri replied with a big smile.

"That's what I like to hear."

"I hope these guys quiet down so I don't get evicted from my apartment for too much noise in the middle of the night," she added as she closed the carrier to contain the bundles of energy. One eviction was enough to worry about, she thought to herself.

"I expect they will," Sam put in, "especially if you fill their big tummies as soon as you get home. I have a sack of the food they've been getting." He pulled the sack from the back of his truck and put it into Terri's car. "The farmer gave it to us. This way they won't have to get used to new food."

"Good idea," Terri agreed.

Turning to Carter with his hand extended, Sam shook his. "It's been nice meeting you, and thanks for your help. It's good that Terri has found someone she can rely on."

"I'm happy to help, and it's good to meet you too. I admire the work you do," Carter told him.

In the car, the puppies were all huddled together and watching everyone moving about. At least they had stopped their constant barking.

"All set?" Carter asked Terri. When she nodded, he closed the SUV's back door and climbed into the passenger seat. Terri said her thanks and good-byes to Sam and stepped up behind the wheel. With a last wave, she drove toward home. The puppies remained quiet with the car in motion.

"I wonder why more people don't know about the work you do as a volunteer?" Carter asked Terri on the way to her apartment.

"Know about my work? Anyone who knows me or who's been in the shop has heard about it. And I've probably asked each one for help feeding the puppies too — though I do wish that more people would actually help out Sam when he needs more hands. There are several of us that he calls on, but he could always use more."

"How does he get his volunteers?"

"I sought him out, but I can't speak for the rest. He investigates each volunteer because he has to be able to completely trust them, or a bad situation could get worse."

At her apartment parking lot, the dogs were too big and rambunctious to be contained in her large basket in which she normally transported puppies upstairs, but Carter had no problem carrying the travel crate with all the puppies safely inside.

"Muscles come in handy. You've saved me a trip up with each of them, one at a time. I never could have lifted that crate."

In her apartment, Terri showed Carter where to clean up in the guest bath off the hall. She did the same in her bedroom bath. Reaching the kitchen ahead of him, she put on water to heat to make hot chocolate that they could sip as they fed and checked each pup.

"Should I close this door to keep them in the kitchen?" he asked moments later.

"I'll get it." Terri picked up Day and Night, who had followed her into the kitchen to see what was going on, and put them in the hall. "Sorry, boys, but these guys are enough to handle without you two trying to get into the act," she said, closing the door.

Carter opened the crate door and the puppies bounded out. They checked out the whole room, sniffing everything as they raced around. He caught one at a time and looked them over.

"I think this one has injured back paws. He's licking them and lifts one whenever he stands," Carter told her after checking out the pup.

Looking at the paws herself, she had to agree. "He must be the last one brought out of the barn. I'll take him to the vet first thing in the morning and have her take a look at him."

When the puppies were all cleaned as well as was possible without taking a bath, Terri put clean blankets and papers in a caged area in the corner of the kitchen that would contain the new guests. Then the feeding process began.

"What can I do to help?" Carter asked.

"Cross your fingers. Sam said they were being weaned, so let's see how they would like a little soupy solid food."

Using the puppy chow from the farmer, she added the mixed formula recommended for puppies this age. She was delighted to see them lapping it up as soon as she put the bowls down.

"Look at them go at it," Carter remarked with a laugh.

"That's good. We don't have to hand feed them from bottles like I do the little guys in the hall."

With the larger puppies contained, Carter opened the kitchen door and walked to the child's large, hard-sided, plastic swimming pool that sat at the end of the hall. The commotion he and Terri had made bringing the Labs in had awakened the little balls of fluff. They were doing their best to stand and look over the edge of the pool to see what was going on in the kitchen. Losing their balance on their hind legs, they bumped into each other and tumbled over one another. That didn't stop each one from jumping up again and trying to stand tall on two feet. Their tiny yips and barks were quiet compared to the noise the larger puppies had made. Now, with full tummies the Labs were the quiet ones.

Squatting by the pool, he gently petted each little one, but that seemed to do nothing to calm them down. In fact, they got more excited as they fought over his attention. He got the idea that they expected him to give them food too.

Walking back into the kitchen, he saw that Terri had removed the empty food bowls and washed them. The Lab puppies had huddled together on a blanket in the corner of their area and were asleep already.

"I think the guys in the hall feel left out."

"One set down and one to go," she said, pulling out three small bottles from the refrigerator that looked very much like baby bottles except much smaller. She heated them briefly in the microwave to take the chill off and then shook and tested each one for the right temperature.

"You don't have to stay and help more, Carter. It's really late," she offered as she worked.

"But if I help, you might get some sleep tonight too. What can I do?"

She met his gaze and smiled. "Thank you. I'll start you with one puppy. With all the practice I've had, I've gotten so I can feed two at once, so this shouldn't take too long with both of us feeding them all at the same time," she told him.

Carter reached for a puppy when she set the bottles on the table, but she stopped him. "Hold it a minute. You'll want this first."

Taking one of the towels piled by the pool, she folded it and handed it to him. "Here, take this and put the puppy on it on your lap. At this age they always seem to be active at both ends at once," she explained with a chuckle. "This should keep you dry."

"You make a good point. Thanks," he said with a wry smile.

While she folded another towel for herself, he nestled a puppy in the middle of his. He took a bottle from the table and experienced bottle-feeding a puppy for the first time. It took a few tries before the puppy really latched on to the nipple and formula still dripped from his mouth.

"He seems to lose as much as he drinks. It's running down his front."

"Yes, but a lot is getting in too," she

replied as she began feeding the two others. "Give him as much as he wants. He'll stop taking it to tell you when he's had enough. And after he eats, he'll lick some from his fur or a sibling will — until they fall asleep, that is."

For a few minutes, the only sounds in the room were the slurps from the tiny dogs as they tried to latch onto the nipples, and a few laughs from the adults trying to feed them.

"How long have you been doing this?" he asked after the puppy he held seemed to get the hang of drinking from the bottle.

Without looking up from her two puppies, she frowned. "How long have I been doing what?"

"How long have you been rescuing puppies?"

"Oh." She shrugged. With the puppies faced away from her, she had wrapped an arm around each one to keep them on her lap and held the bottle out in front of each mouth. She used her palms to keep their little heads tipped up and on target. "I started while I was in college. That's unusual, but a puppy mill was discovered in town and the police closed it down," she began. "My sorority volunteered to take some of the puppies. They were so scrawny

— about as bad as these guys were."

Deep in her happy memories of freeing the puppies from a terrible life, she smiled. "I remember I was about the only one still feeding them when the authorities finally came to get them to give away to good homes they'd found."

"I can see how this might get old really quickly to anyone less devoted to animals than you are."

She laughed. "Are you trying to tell me not to call you again? You've had enough?"

"No, not me, I'm fine. This is sort of fun, and I can see it's important. Frankly, I never realized that it wasn't handled by the paid staff at the vet or the animal shelter."

"There's not enough money to pay for all the help they need. Shelters are always short of volunteers to help. That makes it tough on the animals because they're the very people who can make the animal's life there so much more pleasant. The shelters need people to come and just play with the animals — you know, to walk the dogs and pet the cats. It's tough on them being stuck there."

"Oops, there's no cleaning up for this one," he told her. "He's asleep already, but he drank most of it."

He held up the nearly empty bottle and

Terri smiled. "Good job," she said in an exaggerated praise.

"Thank you, ma'am," he said with a grin. He put the bottle on the table and gently wiped the puppy's chin and neck on the towel.

"This is great," Terri remarked. "These two are about done too, and then I can hope that they'll sleep until my alarm goes off."

While he waited for her to finish, Carter drank the last of his hot chocolate.

"You could warm that up in the micro-wave if you like," Terri offered.

"No, it's good hot or cool," he said, watching her deftly feeding the two puppies.

Cradling the puppies in the folded towels once she'd finished her feedings, Terri and Carter carried them back to the swimming pool that protected the tiles on her hall floor.

"Just leave him on the towel so he'll stay warm," she whispered. "Putting him down on the colder blanket might wake him." Setting down their precious loads close together so they could cuddle for warmth and companionship, Terri straightened and looked up to find him watching her. "I'm awfully glad I had your help. Will your boss let you start the morning a little later so you can get some sleep?"

Carter grinned. Starting to say he was the

boss and could show up pretty much when he wanted to, he quickly drew his lips between his teeth and bit down to keep from talking. This wasn't the time to tell her of his position at M&S. Instead, he just shrugged and then said, "As I said, I've always thought sleep was overrated as a nightly pastime."

His comment made her laugh again, but he noticed her cheeks redden. "I'm glad you called me. This has been fun."

"I can't thank you enough for all your help, Carter. It wouldn't have gone anywhere near as smoothly without you."

"Hey, I'm happy to do it."

She raised her arm to point at the kitchen chair where he'd been sitting. "Don't forget your jacket."

Grabbing it, they walked to the front door. "You don't want any help cleaning up?"

"No, I just have the bottles to wash and refill for the morning so it will be faster than when I'm half asleep," she told him with a grin. "They're finally getting to the point where they can go longer between feedings, which is good 'cause that means I can sleep more now. And I can take them in to work where I have the volunteers to feed them during the day. There are two devoted helpers who show up each morning around opening time when they know we have puppies."

"People come in just to feed the puppies?" he asked as he pulled on his jacket.

She nodded. "If it's not feeding time, they just play with them or sit and pet them. It's very important to get the puppies used to being handled by different people, especially after their unfortunate start in life. After meeting strangers all the time who care for them, they will be friendlier and much less likely to bite when handled as they grow."

"How are these little guys doing?" he asked, looking back at the soundly sleeping balls of fur in the hall.

"I think they're all coming along nicely and will end up making good pets for some families in a few weeks."

He looked back and met her gaze. "Are you always that lucky with them?"

She shook her head and sighed. "No," she said softly. "And the ones I lose are hard to take. Sometimes they're just rescued too late or their treatment before the rescue was too bad, but I always try."

Her eyes sparkled with unshed tears. Stepping closer, Carter gently pulled her against his chest and stroked her back to comfort her. Without hesitation, she put her arms around his waist, which pleased him.

"And you keep on trying. You couldn't do it any other way. I know."

Leaning back, she looked up to meet his gaze. "Could you see those guys over there in such desperate need of help and turn your back and walk away?"

He shook his head and lifted his hands to frame her face. Using his thumbs, he wiped away a tear or two that had found their way down her cheeks. "No, and if you need my help again, day or night, you call me, okay?"

She nodded. "Day or night — I'll do that, thanks," she said softly.

Day and Night, who heard their names, woke enough to look up. Seeing nothing to interest them, they went back to sleep.

"I mean it, Carter. I can't thank you enough."

"No thanks needed," he said softly as he lowered his head until his lips brushed against hers. Raising his head a few inches and seeing no resistance on her part, he pressed his lips against her soft ones and twisted slowly as if to get more comfortable.

The sudden awareness that her lips felt very warm and soft under his shocked him. The fragrance of sweet chocolate from the drink earlier tantalized him. The fact that he liked kissing her, liked spending time with her, just plain liked her, suddenly hit him like a four-by-four whacking him on the side of the head. It was enough of a surprise to make him end the kiss. He raised his head and their gazes locked. He even liked that she looked as dazed as he felt.

What was going on? He'd set out to help her rescue some puppies, but he was the one who needed rescuing now. *Perfect,* he thought. *Fall for the woman and then have a problem with her in your shopping development. Yeah, that would work real well.*

His backbone stiffened as his practical side took over. Smiling, he said, "Sleep well." Adding a good night, he got out of there — because he needed to get home to get some sleep, he told himself. He didn't want to think that he really had wanted to stay and kiss her again. It must be from getting so little sleep. Tomorrow, he hoped, he could think straighter and not feel such a strong, irrational attraction to her. Sleep, that's what he needed — some sleep.

Terri watched him stride down the hall outside her apartment without even a glance back, and then she closed and locked the door after him.

She ran her fingertips over her lips. Their kiss had been so sweet, but then he'd seemed to freeze up and leave. She leaned against the inside of the door and sighed.

Night and Day pattered down the hall, as they always did when the door opened or shut, their nails tapping on the tiles. "What do you guys think? Maybe that was a good-bye kiss instead of a good night kiss." Leaning down, she petted them both. "Come on, boys, it's bedtime — finally."

Checking all the nightlights she always left on to reassure the puppies that they were in a safe place, she headed for a shower. She was asleep moments after her hair was dry and her head finally hit the pillow.

The following morning Terri had just finished feeding all the pups when she heard the knock on her door. Her brow knitted in a frown and she drew her lower lip between her teeth and bit down as she went to answer the knock. She hoped it wasn't her landlord telling her that the puppies had made too much noise that morning or that she had made too much noise coming and going the night before.

Looking through the spy hole in the door, she heaved a sigh of relief as she quickly opened it.

"Who'd you think it was, the puppy police?" her neighbor and good friend Marty said. In a suit and coat, she was dressed for work, her purse on her shoulder.

Terri laughed. "Well, these guys did get a little excited this morning."

Marty spotted the puppies and went down the hall to kneel beside the kiddie pool. Petting them, she cooed and laughed at the antics of each one. Hearing a noise in the kitchen, she looked up to see the Labs. "Okay, now that makes more sense. I couldn't imagine these little guys were the ones barking this morning."

"Oh, they were until I fed them, but I'm sure it was the Labs you heard."

"How do you do it? I hardly have time to dress and do my hair in the morning, and you have puppies to feed and cart to the car before you can leave for work."

"Well, it helps that my shop doesn't open until ten, but I do have to get the new ones to the vet this morning. I'm worried that one has burned paws."

While Marty switched her attentions to the Labs, Terri told her the whole story of the night before.

"Wow, I can't believe I never heard a thing," she responded with a laugh.

"I hope the same can be said for the rest of our neighbors."

"Listen, they think so highly of what you are doing that they would never complain.

The rest of us would make life too hard for them too."

Terri thanked her friend. "I wish I had someone to stick up for me at work too."

"You're the boss. How can anyone complain about the puppies there?"

Terri shook her head. "I haven't had a chance to tell you. I'm being evicted from Riverside."

"They can't do that. Your shop is so popular."

Terri shrugged. "I can't get them to see it that way, but as soon as I get these guys settled there this morning, I'm going to contact an attorney."

"I hope it doesn't come to that," Marty told her.

"It already has. They say the other shops are complaining about me."

"They must be jealous." She shook her head. "You let me know what happens. There must be something you can do. Let me know if there's anything I can do, okay?"

"Thanks, Marty. I'll let you know as soon as I learn anything."

Her friend leaned toward her to give her a supportive hug and then walked back to the apartment door.

"Hey, you wouldn't want to carry a basket of tiny puppies to the car on your way, would you?"

"Sure," Marty said with a laugh.

Terri packed them all in the rear of her SUV in just three trips to the apartment with Marty's help with the basket. Hitting the vet's just before they opened, she got them to let her in with the puppy she suspected of having burned paws. The vet assured her that the burns were only slight and would heal without any treatment.

"She'd probably lick anything you put on it anyway."

Happy with the good news, she drove on to her shop. Making some quick changes in the cage arrangement to accommodate the larger puppies, she managed to get them all settled by the time Sue arrived. Leaving her in charge of the shop, Terri went to her office to call the attorney.

The phone call couldn't have been more frustrating. She learned that he would not take her case against M&S Development Company.

"My caseload is just too big right now," he said, but it sounded like an excuse, not a reason.

She knew that he had helped other shop owners with their leases too, and she suspected that he didn't want to go up against M&S. In the long run, he could lose business if M&S refused to deal with renters using him as their attorney. Terri couldn't fault him, though she was disappointed. It was his decision to make, but it made her problem seem bigger. She had to find an attorney and he was the only one she'd had experience with.

Knowing nothing about any other attorney, she left her office and walked out into the shop. She wanted to ask Sue more about the attorney-neighbor she had mentioned. As it turned out, Sue was a fount of information about the man. His office was downtown, he was in a long-standing partnership with one other attorney, and he shopped at the same grocery store as Sue because she had seen him there often.

"I'd rather use him than picking one by throwing a dart at the open phonebook," Terri told her.

"Do you want me to call him now? Or you could call and say that I recommended him." She shrugged. "He might see you today."

"As tired as I am today after little sleep last night, I'll just wait until you talk to him while he mows tomorrow. If he's taking on new cases, just let me know and I'll call his office Monday for an appointment."

"Sure thing. He's real nice. I think you'll

like him, and I think you can trust his opinion of what you should do."

"That's good to know."

Terri sighed and then suddenly cried out with surprise as a little black Lab puppy raced by her feet. "Oh, no you don't," she said, chasing him. He ran to the shelf of treats and stood with his paws on the shelf as he nosed at the packages.

Lifting him into her arms before he'd gotten a package in his mouth, she turned to see how he'd escaped from the enclosure when a customer approached her looking very sheepish.

"I'm so sorry he got away," the gray-haired woman said. "He slipped out of my grip and jumped off my lap. I couldn't get up from the floor where I was playing with him fast enough to catch him," she added with a laugh. "I'm not as agile as I used to be."

"No harm done, and now we know he's got a great nose," Terri assured her with a laugh. "I may have to consider a puppy-height fence around the carpeted area to contain them when they aren't in the dog cage."

"That's a good idea. I love helping, but I worry about the little imps getting loose." Smiling, the woman fiddled with her purse but made no move to leave. "Um, forgive me if I'm speaking out of turn, but I heard a rumor that you are being evicted from this shop location. Can that possibly be true?" she asked.

"I wish I could tell you a different answer," Terri told her with no hesitation. "But, yes, M&S Development Company has served me with an eviction notice."

"Oh, no," she said.

"But I'm fighting it," Terri quickly added.

"But why would they do that? Your shop is so popular," she said. "I just love coming here to play with the puppies. I've always wanted to have one, but there are no pets allowed in my apartment building."

Two other customers, who had heard their conversation, moved closer nodding their agreement. "Anyone I know who has a dog knows about you. The dog food you sell is so much better than the stuff at the big discount stores or grocery stores. My dog thrives on it," one said.

Terri smiled. "I'm glad, and thanks. I admit that I wish I knew the answer to that one too," she replied. "The closest reason I can guess for the eviction is that they thought from the baking equipment we had to install in the kitchen that this was a people bakery, not a dog-treat one."

"But what's wrong with having a dog bakery? My dog loves all your treats, and I feel better knowing exactly what is in each one," another customer put in. "I don't like to feed him preservatives if I don't have to."

"Well," Terri said, "you all keep thinking good thoughts and that should help the next time I see them about the eviction."

Sue joined them with a tray full of little bags of fresh treats she planned to put on the shelf near them. "Terri's going to talk to an attorney Monday," she offered. "So you gotta keep those good thoughts until then."

"We will, dear," the older woman said.

"Oh, those are just the treats I was looking for," another customer said. "When I saw the shelf was empty, I thought I'd play with the puppies for a while. I hoped you'd be bringing out some more."

Sue held out the tray, and the customers helped themselves to nearly half the bags of treats. "Let me just set this tray down and I'll meet you at the check-out counter," she promised.

When those customers had left with their purchases, no one else entered the shop for a while. Terri saw Sue heading her way after she finished emptying the tray of treats onto the shelves.

"I'm so sorry," Sue said. "I apologize. I

shouldn't have said all that to the customers without asking how much you wanted people to know."

"It's all right," Terri replied with a dismissive gesture with her hand. "I'd rather have them know the facts than believe rumors and half-truths. In fact, I think customer support could be a good tool in my arsenal to fight M&S."

"It's got to be. They want a business in here that draws customers, and if you show them how many customers support your staying here, it should work in your favor."

"At this point I'll take all the help I can get." Terri sat on the floor and lifted out one of the little puppies. "These little guys always make me feel better, but the future looks as bleak for them as it does for me."

"What do you mean?" Sue asked. "They're doing great."

"Yes, but if I lose the shop and have to get a regular job somewhere to recoup the money I will have lost, it's these guys who will suffer. I won't be able to help rescue more like them because I couldn't leave them at home during the day all alone."

"Gosh, I hadn't thought of that, but you're right. No office is going to let you bring puppies in with you."

"No, and I can't leave them home. The

puppies couldn't go eight or nine hours between feedings, and Night and Day couldn't go that long between walks outside. Oh, dear — I'm not even sure I could keep Night and Day."

"Don't think that yet. My attorney friend, Blake, has just got to have a good idea that will keep you here," Sue insisted.

"I hope so. Can you call me after you've talked to him tomorrow? Then I'll know to save the time to see him Monday if he can fit me in."

"Sure thing." She held up her hands with her fingers crossed for good luck and smiled.

The little bell over the door rang and Sue went to wait on the new customer as Terri continued to play with the puppies, each one in turn. Sitting comfortably on the floor, she was glad her customers didn't expect her to wear business attire. Dressed daily in a casual style of slacks and sweaters now that fall was here, she felt she looked nice enough and she could handle the puppies too — no expensive suit to worry about ruining.

"This is going to be a long weekend, guys. It'll be just all of you and me, plus Night and Day, of course, so I'm counting on you to cheer me up the way you always do."

As if he had understood every word, the

puppy in her hands licked her chin.

"Of course you will," she said with a laugh, holding his little warm body gently against her chest.

CHAPTER FIVE

On Saturday morning the doorbell rang just as Terri had gotten dressed and was padding toward the kitchen to feed the pups. Thinking it was Marty, she flung the door open. Startled, she stared at Carter who stood with a white bakery box in his hands.

"Good morning," he said with a grin. "Am I too early to bring you breakfast?"

"Not with puppies here that won't let me sleep any longer," she replied. "Come on in. I was just going to put coffee on. Would you like some?"

"I'd love it," he said.

They walked to the kitchen where he put the box on the small table and turned to watch her fill the drip coffeemaker.

"I see I'm in time to help feed the stock," he said.

Terri looked at all the puppies, standing against the sides of their enclosures, vying for their attention and looking for food.

"What gave you your first clue?"

He laughed and stepped over to pet the Labs. "These guys look like they're doing just fine."

Terri prepared the Labs' morning feeding and carried two of the bowls to their enclosure. When Carter saw that they were ready, he did the same with the remaining two. For a few moments they watched the puppies noisily slurp up their food. But the whining from the hall sent Terri to the refrigerator to prepare the little ones' breakfast. After that feeding, she and Carter washed up side by side at the double sink in the kitchen.

"Now is it time for you to get some sustenance?" he asked as they dried their hands.

"Now would be great."

"I hope you like bagels and cream cheese with jelly."

"Mmm, yeah, I love 'em."

"I brought four kinds of jelly, and I even grabbed a couple pots of peanut butter in case you prefer that."

"Having so much choice makes this a gourmet breakfast in my opinion," Terri told him.

She put two dishes on the table and got out knives and napkins to put on the table as well. Returning to the counter, she poured a cup of coffee for each of them. "Do you take cream or sugar?"

"No thanks, I don't want anything to stand between me and the caffeine," he replied with a laugh.

For a few minutes they read the names of each of the jellies in the little inch-high bottles and made their selections. "Where did you find this treat?"

"I picked it up at the hotel coffee shop. I sometimes eat there for breakfast and thought I'd bring some to share with you after helping with the puppies."

She met his gaze and smiled. "That's very sweet of you, Carter. You're a very caring person and . . . and I'm glad I met you," she said softly.

"I'm glad I met you too," he responded, and Terri was glad that it didn't sound like he had responded in kind just to be polite. He'd sounded like he really meant it.

"So what do you do on your Saturday off from work?" she asked after swallowing another bite of the light bagel with cream cheese and raspberry jam.

He shrugged. "I rarely have the day off. I'm busy at work now with a project that's due November first. Until that's done, it's kind of all work and little play."

"But you have to eat, and it's fun to share with you."

"What about you? What do you do?"

"Well, sometimes I have to work if my weekend person can't make it. Otherwise, I'm delighted to stay home and clean the apartment, and lug laundry up and down the elevator to the laundry room in the basement. I tell you, it's an exciting life I lead."

He laughed. "You know, you may look at your life as less than exciting, but every puppy you've saved is very excited about it." He wiped his mouth with the paper napkin and dropped it onto his empty plate.

"Yeah, I guess you're right, but I couldn't do it without help from my friends. Thank you for surprising me with your help this morning."

One hand leaning on the table, he watched her and smiled.

"What are you thinking?"

"I'm just thinking about other women I know who would have hit the ceiling if I'd dropped in at this early an hour on a Saturday morning. In fact, they probably would have still been asleep, not up and dressed like you were." He shook his head. "And the thought of my seeing them without makeup would have sent them over the edge."

It was Terri's turn to laugh. "Maybe I should apologize for not being more like them, but what you see is what I am. Oh, I enjoy putting on makeup to go out looking my best, but I'm more comfortable in these worn sweats with no makeup."

"That's one of the things I like best about you. You have no pretense. You're happy with who you are."

Carter suddenly realized that the conversation was getting too close to what he didn't want to talk about. She knew little of who he really was, and he didn't want to take a chance and tell her now where he worked. He rose and helped carry the remainders of their breakfast to the counter.

"Why don't you keep all the little jars of jam and peanut butter? I don't think we emptied any of them."

"I'll have gourmet toast every day next week," she replied with a grin.

"Good. Well, I'd better get on to the office. My work doesn't seem to get done when I'm not there."

She smiled. "No, I've noticed mine doesn't either."

They walked together to the front door, stopping on the way to pet the pups that were still awake.

"Thanks for breakfast, Carter."

He turned to her at the door. "Then you really don't mind that I stop by bearing food?"

"You're welcome to do that anytime — anytime."

"I'll remember that." And with that he left.

That afternoon Terri received the promised call from Sue, who never worked at the shop on Saturdays so she could stay home with her family. Terri worked the full day with a teenaged part-time clerk, Tony Barrett, who worked just weekends for her. She also had a woman who normally worked weekends too. She had reentered the work force after retiring and finding herself bored sitting at home. Terri worked when the woman's grandkids came for a weekend visit like this weekend, or when she went to see them. It was a small price to pay to have a capable woman she could easily leave in charge on Saturdays and Sundays.

"I talked to Blake just now," Sue said in her call to Terri at the shop. "I found him mowing his lawn right when I said he would be."

"Will he see me about the lease?" Terri asked, getting right to the point.

"Yes, he said that if you got to his office at eight-thirty in the morning, he would have time to talk to you before his first appointment came in at nine."

"Oh, Sue, that's great. Thank you so much for talking to him," Terri told her.

"I'm happy to do it, especially when he promised to work you in instead of making you wait for an open appointment. I put in an extra plug and told him that saving your shop means saving my job that I like a lot," she replied cheerily. "I've got my fingers crossed that he can work a miracle."

"Then you can open the shop Monday? I might be later than ten by the time I go home after I talk to him to pick up the puppies."

"That's no problem. You can count on me. Oh, and by the way, I didn't tell him much more than you had received an eviction notice you didn't deserve."

Terri smiled and felt good at the solid backing. "Thanks for your support, Sue."

"We're all counting on you to keep the store open," Sue replied, adding to the responsibility Terri felt.

After ending the call, Terri swung up her fist in a silent "yes" cheer. The attorney would see her. Smiling with optimism, she went to check on the customers playing with

109

the puppies. The Lab puppies' eagerness to romp made them so cute she had to laugh. At the rate they were growing, they would need more space in no time. It was a good thing they would be going back to their farm before then. Right now, though she was inviting chaos, she wanted them all to have more room to play. She sat on the floor and opened the gate to their confined area.

"That was good news on the phone, guys," she said to them, throwing a pair of knotted socks across the floor and watching as the puppies all ran for it and brought it back toward her. The race developed into a tug of war. One was always odd dog out. That one raced from one sibling to another trying to get a sock away from them. At that rate it didn't take much exercise to tire them all out. Soon they'd had enough and were climbing on her legs to be petted.

Leaning against a cabinet, she and two teenaged customers, who had come in during the fun, did their best to give them equal attention. Soon their big dark eyes drooped and when she put them back into their space that they had come to consider home, they were quickly asleep.

"You make having a puppy look so easy. I wish my mom could see you in action," one of the teenagers said. "She won't let us have a dog 'cause she says they're too much work."

"Yeah, she's always saying that if we learn to be responsible about keeping our rooms clean, then she'll consider getting a dog." She groaned and rolled her eyes to let Terri know what she thought of her mom's bargain.

"Dogs do take attention on a regular schedule," Terri hedged.

"Yeah, Mom said we couldn't sleep in anymore because the dog would have to be taken out at the same time each morning," one of the girls said with a laugh.

"It's easier coming to play with your puppies," the other said. "This way I can sleep in."

Terri shook her head a little later when the girls wandered out the door. Their mother had to be a wise woman to realize that most of the work of having a dog would fall on her own shoulders. Without knowing any more about them, it did seem better that the girls came in and played with the puppies instead of getting one themselves.

Checking to be sure the low gate was securely latched to keep the puppies confined when they woke, Terri rose and watched them sleep for a few moments. The way they piled on top of each other when they slept always amused her. It didn't seem to matter if another pup's hind quarters were draped over their back, they just wanted to be close together for warmth, security, and companionship.

She felt a tinge of jealousy as she was reminded how alone she'd felt lately. She was terribly busy with the shop and the puppies, but her biological clock was ticking. She wanted to find someone with whom to move beyond puppy love. She smiled. Her time would come. An image of Carter flashed into her mind. She really didn't know much about him, other than the fact that he liked dogs. But then she wanted to believe that a man who liked dogs and owned one who was as well mannered as Fred had to be a good man.

With another smile for the puppies, she headed for her cleaning supplies. Business was always light during the late Saturday afternoon hours. She imagined everyone home getting ready for dinner or to go out on a Saturday night date. For her, it was the best time to clean the shop. She would start on the opposite side and finish with the vacuuming that would surely wake the puppies. That way, soon after they woke, it would be about time for them all to go home.

As she dusted the shelves as well as waited on the few customers that Tony couldn't handle alone, she couldn't help but wonder if Carter would call her. Or what if she called him? "Carter, how would you like to take me to dinner?" she practiced silently. She frowned and began again. "Carter, how would you like to go to dinner with me?"

"Did you say something?" Tony asked.

Terri laughed. "No, sorry, I was just talking to myself. It's been a long week."

He smiled and went back to straightening the packages as he restocked the shelves.

Terri went back to thinking about Carter.

To her delight, Terri didn't have to wait even twenty-four hours to see Carter again. It was late afternoon Sunday when she had just gotten settled after taking Night and Day and the Lab puppies out for a walk. Her doorbell rang and announced his unexpected arrival. She opened the door with a grin on her face. In one hand he carried a huge picnic basket and a picnic blanket was draped over the other.

"Sorry I didn't call first. May I come in anyway?" he asked with a grin.

"Of course. You could guess I'd be here. There isn't enough time between feedings and walking these guys to go anywhere

113

except for quick trips to the grocery store," she replied.

Walking directly into the living room, he deposited the things he carried on the coffee table. "I hope you haven't eaten supper yet."

"No, it's about time to feed my little brood. I was going to do that first and then select which can of soup I would like to heat for tonight's culinary treat," she said with a grin.

"Then I'm just in time. I hope you won't be too disappointed without canned soup when you see what I've brought."

He pulled off his jacket and looked very much at home in his worn jeans hugging his muscular legs and a maroon sweater that looked soft. Terri wished she hadn't picked her most stained pair of jeans to wear today. But then, because Carter had helped with a rescue, he had seen them before anyway.

Once she'd cleared the few things from the coffee table and set them on the end table, he set down the picnic basket and opened it. Lifting out a tablecloth, he laid it double thickness over the polished surface and then set the basket on top of it again, this time at the end.

The fragrance of a blend of foods wafted up at her. She inhaled deeply. "Smells delicious," she said with a broad smile.

"Wait until you taste it."

A spread of food grew as he pulled out crispy fried chicken tenders, potato salad, and two individual salads of fresh greens topped with chopped vegetables and grape tomatoes.

A pitcher of raspberry tea with a center cylinder filled with ice followed. Two tall plastic thermal glasses, and plastic plates, and flatware emptied the basket except for a white box that he put back in on the bottom.

"This will do us until dessert," he said, setting the basket aside. "I hope you see something that you like."

"I don't see anything that I don't like," she insisted with a laugh. "And a picnic in October is special fun."

Day and Night smelled something they liked too, as they nosed around the coffee table.

"Oh, no you don't," Carter said to them as he held his hand out between their noses and the food.

"Kitchen," Terri ordered. The dogs looked at her as if they didn't believe that she would send them away from such a feast, but when she said it a second time, they went into the kitchen, turned around, and laid down with their heads on their paws right in the kitchen door frame. "Good dogs," she praised in their direction. "Stay."

"Do you see that? They're not totally devoid of manners," she told him.

He smiled. "Shall we sit on the floor or on the couch?" he asked.

"With all the bending over I've done already today, how about if we sit on the floor and lean against the couch?"

"That sounds perfect," he agreed. "We can pretend we're sitting on grass and leaning against a tree."

"It'll be a lovely picnic without the ants," she put in with a smile.

They sat on the floor, Carter's legs stretched out beside the table and Terri's folded between the couch and the table.

"Oops, I almost forgot," he said, reaching to open the basket again. "Here you go," he added as he pulled out two napkins that matched the tablecloth from an elastic under the top and handed one to her.

"This is a wonderful treat — such wonderful service, and with a smile that makes me want to smile."

"That's my motto," he said, " 'service with a smile.' "

"I think someone else beat you to that slogan."

He shrugged. "I'll just borrow it for the day. So if you've got anything to keep you from smiling, just forget it for the rest of today."

"That sounds like a plan," she said, wishing she could so easily forget that she might be out of business by the middle of November.

"Great — now what may I serve you?" he asked, picking up one of the plates and filling it according to her directions. He poured her a glass of tea and set it in front of her. "Do you need a sweetener in your tea?"

"No, I drink it straight," she replied with a grin.

Once he'd gotten his own food and drink, they relaxed back against the couch and began to eat their picnic supper.

"I like this picnic site. We have no mosquitoes," he said moments later.

"But it lacks much in the way of scenery — no woods, no stream, no open sky over us."

"You're right, but we have plenty of wildlife. Where else could we eat with so many brown eyes watching our every move?"

Terri looked up to see the puppies in the hall and the ones they could see through the kitchen door were all awake and watching them.

"Hmm, I guess all of them have noses that work."

"How long do you figure we have before they all bark to be fed too?" he asked.

She groaned. "Eat fast. It won't be long. When they start making noise, I'll have to stop and feed them," she answered. "Oh, but this is too good to rush. Mmm," she said enjoying the salad, "this dressing is so good."

"Wait until you see dessert."

"Do I get a hint?" she asked.

In just a few minutes, a chorus of complaints about empty stomachs was beginning from the owners of all those eyes watching them eat. The humans in the apartment had to laugh.

"The little ones have probably never seen a person eating before, but I really think they know what we're doing and want some too," Terri said after finishing a piece of chicken that was both crispy and moist. "What do you think? Could you interrupt your supper and eat the rest after we feed them?"

Popping the remainder of a chicken tender into his mouth, he chewed and swallowed it. "Well, since they show no sign of quieting down, I think we'd better feed them before your neighbors start pounding on the walls."

"You can mix up the mush for the Labs while I heat the bottles to the right temperature."

They rose to their feet and headed to the kitchen. With words of assurance that their supper was coming soon, the dogs quieted a bit and watched the preparation with interest.

"How long before the little ones get the mush?" Carter asked.

"It won't be long. Once they started getting fed on a regular basis, they started growing fast."

"Giving them all the mush should be easier on you."

"Yes, it's much faster without the bottles, but I still have to feed each one individually to make sure each gets his or her nourishment. Otherwise the fastest eater gets more."

"Okay, I've got it."

Terri noted that, with few instructions from her, Carter had the mush mixed in no time and divided into the separate dishes for the Labs.

"What do you think? Take the Labs out one at a time? Will the others stand for that if they see one eating?"

Terri laughed at the image of the chaos that would produce. "I take them out one at a time, but set him at one of the bowls and then get the next one right away. Then when they're done, we get to play 'catch the puppies' and put them all back."

He laughed at the image.

Terri was thankful that Carter picked up a bottle and helped with the third little puppy when he had the Lab pups at their bowls. But the Labs were done licking their empty bowls clean before the bottles were empty.

Moving his chair to the kitchen door where he could sit and stretch out his legs, he kept the feisty pups from leaving the kitchen and heading for their chicken. He'd finally finished feeding the little ball of fur in his hands long after Terri was done with her two.

Stepping over his legs, she put those little ones back in their temporary home in the hall. Meanwhile, the Labs climbed all over each other to be the center of her attention.

"It's amazing how much these dogs can do to help their masters when they've finished with their training." One of the pups tugged at her shoelaces and succeeded in untying her jogging shoe. "And it's amazing how much mischief they can get into at this age."

"How is the puppy we suspected had been burned?"

"The vet said she was fine. It was only as bad as sunburn. She no longer seems affected by it."

"That was lucky. Have you heard how their mother is doing?"

"They treated her burns and are watching her for the effects of smoke inhalation, but she seems fine. The vet said the owners were taking her home on Wednesday, so I'll take the Lab puppies out there Wednesday morning before the shop opens. They'll be there when she arrives home. I don't want her to worry about them even for a minute longer."

"That should be a happy reunion."

"Yes, but it sure is going to be quiet around here," she replied with a laugh. "My neighbors will probably love it."

"How long will you have these little guys?"

"They'll be with me for at least two more weeks, maybe three. It depends on how they do."

"There, it's all gone," Carter said proudly as he set down the empty bottle. "And I think the size of his little tummy just doubled," he added with a laugh.

"To bed with him then," Terri said as she set all the bottles and dishes to soak in soapy water in the sink.

The dogs taken care of, she washed her hands carefully and moved over to give Carter room to do the same.

"Raising puppies is a lot of work without the mother to nurse them," he said.

"It's a lot of work even with her. And it's expensive too, with all the visits to the vet for the shots, etcetera. People who get into raising puppies thinking they can make easy money by letting nature take its course are sadly mistaken. And when they fail to keep up with all the work and care, the dogs are the ones who suffer."

They stood by the sink drying their hands on opposite ends of her hand towel. As she hung it up over the towel ring, he raised a dry hand to cradle her jaw. She looked up and their gazes met.

"These puppies are very lucky to have you to look after them." He smiled. "And I'm very glad I ran into you on the jogging path."

"Me too," she agreed softly. Not comfortable with the seriousness of his comments, she added with a laugh, "You saved me from some scrapes and bruises, for which I thank you very much, you know."

"You're very welcome."

As if he'd been reading her mind, he leaned down and kissed her smile. His lips were soft and warm and wonderful. Sliding her arms around his waist and leaning lightly against him, she convinced herself that she had misread his motivation when he left so abruptly the other night. He was most definitely interested in her.

He kissed her again, nipping at her lower lip, and then straightened.

"Um, was that thunder in the distance I heard near our picnic grounds?" she asked in the silence.

"Hmm, it could be a storm, but I could have sworn that the temperature here was rising and not falling."

Smiling, he put his arm around her shoulders. Holding her against his side, he ushered her back to their picnic. "We'd better finish eating our picnic supper before it rains."

"I think I've worked up an appetite for a little more potato salad."

"Your wish is my command," he said, serving her another spoonful.

"Thanks, but that's enough," she said, when he started to serve a second spoonful. "Got to save room for the mystery dessert."

The dessert in the white box was well worth saving room for. When the time came, he served them each several little profiteroles with creamy dark chocolate sauce.

"This has all been so good," she said later as they cleaned up and repacked the picnic basket. "You either went to an excellent culinary institute, or you must tell me where you got it all."

"I'll do better than that. It's all from my favorite restaurant, and I'll take you there next Friday night for dinner. How's that?"

"Mmm, that sounds like an offer I wouldn't want to refuse," she replied with a smile.

"That's good." He slid the back of his knuckles down her temple to her cheek. "Listen, as much as I'd like to stay, I've got to get home to finish some drawings for the morning. Thanks for eating with me."

"I'm the one to thank you for bringing it. That was really sweet."

"Then you don't mind that I came without calling first?"

"I'll forgive you this time because of the yummy dinner," she said with a grin. "And next time too," she added as she closed the basket, "even without dessert."

Laughing, they walked down the hall side by side. Setting the basket on the floor by the door, he shrugged into his jacket.

"See you Friday for dinner then," she said. "What time should I be ready?"

"Can I call you with the time when I get a

reservation?"

"Sure — I'll feed the little guys just before we leave so they'll be good for enough time to eat."

He opened the door and picked up the basket. "Okay, they're closed on Mondays, so I'll call Tuesday morning and then call you."

Before she could verbally agree with more than a smile, he left her apartment.

After closing and locking the door, she danced her way down the hall toward the kitchen. Not understanding the dance but joining in the fun, Night and Day circled her, vying for her attention.

How could she feel so good about seeing Carter again at the same time that she felt so bad with her eviction problem at work looming over her?

Sitting erectly in the chair facing the desk in the attorney's office, Terri needed only ten minutes to explain all her contacts with M&S Development Company leading up to signing the lease for K-Nine Treats.

Dressed in her dark-gray suit with a white blouse, she sat quietly while attorney Blake Roberts read every word of her lease. She watched his bowed gray head as he concentrated on the fine print.

When he finished reading, he pulled off his reading glasses and dropped them onto his desk pad and leaned back in his seat. "Well, as far as I can tell, everything you have said is substantiated with this lease, Ms. Bookman, though I would have worded it a little more clearly."

Terri felt a smile blooming on her face as her heart raced. She didn't dare move her hands that were tightly gripped together on her lap because she knew they would tremble with nervousness.

"Other than your wanting it clearer, that's exactly what I wanted to hear," she said. "I couldn't bear to go back and rent downtown from my previous landlord again, though I know the space is still empty."

"Didn't you do well there?"

"I didn't do badly as far as the business was concerned, though business at Riverside is much better. But the reason I moved was the landlord. He had six hands — two stole from me every chance he got, and the other four hands were always trying to grope me. I definitely want him to remain as a thing of the past."

She shook her head. "Other than my apartment, which I have no trouble with, that was my first renting experience, and it taught me plenty. I learned never to trust a landlord and to get everything in writing. That's why I hired an attorney to write the contract that you just read. I never tried to mislead M&S as they claim, and I want very much to stay in business there."

"I can appreciate that, but . . ." Pausing, he straightened in his seat and picked up the lease again.

"That 'but' doesn't sound very good."

"No, I'm afraid what else I have to say is not good. You see, if you fought the eviction notice, attorney and court costs would be very expensive. While I think you're in the right, proving it in front of a judge might not be as easy as convincing me has been."

"But that's not fair."

"I know, but I'm telling you this because it's important to realize what you are getting into. You will have to pay for my investigator's charge to get statements from all the other shop owners at Riverside to see if they stick with their complaints, or at the threat of a court appearance, fold. We'll have to subpoena the plans that M&S made for the space and study how they conflict with what you are doing there, and what they thought you would do."

"And that will take time."

"Yes, that's right. You'll have to appear in court when the case comes up on the docket, and that's where M&S can run up your costs rapidly. I'm sure they have an attorney on their payroll, and he can ask for a continuance and recesses until" — he spread out his hands palms up — "until fighting this eviction costs you more than all you have invested in your shop. You could stand to lose it all and end up with more new legal costs."

The starch gone from her backbone, Terri collapsed against the back of her chair. "All that work and all that money — gone?"

"I'm sorry, but the best advice I could give you now is quickly find another location and move before your time is up. If you're late vacating the premises, they can even keep your security deposit against additional rent."

"But I'm in the right in this matter."

"I'm sorry, Ms. Bookman. The good guys don't always win. M&S knows you don't qualify for free legal aide, and I'm sure they don't expect you to hire anyone to help fight this notice because they know what it would cost you."

Nodding, she rose on wobbly legs. "Mr. Snyder did look surprised when I said that I would fight it. Well, thank you for seeing me so quickly. Just send your bill to the shop."

He grinned and came around the desk to

hand her back her lease papers. "Now, there I have some good news. I don't charge for an initial consultation, especially not when I'm doing a good neighbor a favor. I only charge if I take the case."

"That's a blessing," she said, extending her hand to shake his. "Thank you."

"I wish you luck, Ms. Bookman. Sue never stops singing your praises. She almost makes me wish we owned a dog so we could frequent your shop."

Terri smiled at his humor. "Thank you."

"I hope you find a spot for your shop that will work just as well as Riverside."

Terri nodded but couldn't talk past the lump that was growing in her throat. She turned and left his office, trying to smile at the receptionist who wished her a good day.

Going home and changing before she packed up the puppies made her feel a little better. Returning to the shop, she found a parking space right behind her end of the row of shops and restaurants. She turned off the motor and stayed behind the wheel staring at the side of her shop. Because it was at the end of the line of stores, she had two windows on the side in addition to the big ones on the front facing the river. The light from the front one lit the side of the shop area while the back one gave Tom natural daylight in the kitchen.

If only they would let her add a side entrance so her customers with dogs would never have to enter the front walkway, then the other shop owners couldn't complain and the no-dogs policy wouldn't hurt her. She sat up straight. That would work, she thought happily.

No it wouldn't, she thought then, slumping back in the seat. She sighed. It wouldn't solve the problem of not having a people-food bakery that M&S wanted there. And the health department wouldn't let her bake for humans and dogs in the same kitchen. The rules were entirely different, and when it came right down to it, she didn't even want to bake for human consumption.

Getting depressed, which never solved any problem, she climbed out of the car. Leading the Labs and Night and Day on their leashes, she lifted out the basket of puppies. Locking the car with a click on her remote control on her keychain, she entered the shop through the back door and greeted Tom on her way through the kitchen to her office. He looked at her expectantly, but the explanation of what happened would come after she had put away the menagerie.

M&S may get her out, but they couldn't get her down, she vowed.

When she finally had all the dogs in their places, she was surprised to see there were at least twenty people in the small shop.

"Terri," Sue called from the register, "these people are all here to see you."

Terri looked around to see the customers and Sue looking at her expectantly. Even Tom had come out from the kitchen.

"What happened?" Terri asked with a worried frown on her forehead. "What's wrong now?"

CHAPTER SIX

Terri stood still and watched as the customers merged into a circle around her.

"That's what we want to know. What happened?" one of her regular customers finally asked. "Word has gotten around about you getting an eviction notice, and we came to show our support."

"And we want to see what we can do to help you fight it," another put in.

Terri's mouth opened in surprise as she looked at each one in the group. Most were nodding their heads in agreement.

"Your store is so different, and you care so much about the health of our pets that we want to help," a supporter said.

"And don't forget all the work she does to save those little puppies," another said to those around her. Turning back to Terri, she added, "You've earned all the help we can give."

"It's time the big guys stopped stomping

on the little guys," a man at the rear, whom Terri had seen in the shop a few times, added.

Tears burned in her eyes that she blinked away, but this time they were tears of joy and happiness. "I can't imagine a better bunch of customers than you all. I can't tell you what it means to have your support, but . . ." Her words faded and she shrugged.

"But?" Sue asked. "What did Blake . . . what did the lawyer have to say?"

Terri took a deep breath for fortification for the explanation. "Actually, he said that while I'm right, in that I never tried to state anything but the truth in the lease — well, despite that, he advised me to give up and look for another location. He thought that M&S could stall and ultimately cost me more money than all I have invested already. I just can't afford that."

Several customers gasped audibly. "Oh, he can't mean it," one said.

"But where are you going to go?" another asked.

"What can we do to help?" yet another asked.

Terri held up her hand to stop the flow of questions and comments that continued. "I love it here in this location, but I just can't afford to fight the eviction. I'm not ready to give up my business though. I'm going to start looking for another place, but first I'm going to try to reason with the rental agent at M&S once more. I have to at least try now that I have an attorney's opinion that I'm in the right."

The group of men and women applauded. "You go, girl," one woman said.

"When are you going over there? Can you go see the M&S guy today? We'll stay and help with the puppies all afternoon if we have to," the woman's friend offered. The two women nodded in agreement.

By this time, the noise of so many voices had awakened the little puppies, and they all voiced their support in their high-pitched barks.

"Feeding time?" Terri asked Sue.

"What gave you your first clue?" Sue joked as she glanced at the feeding schedule for each bunch. "Close enough, and I don't think they'll quiet down without feeding now," she said with a laugh.

"Oh, can I feed one of the little ones?" an older woman asked. "My friend Marjorie has been here twice and can't stop telling me how much fun it is. We can't have any pets where I live, and I hoped to come here and help often like she does. Now it looks like I won't be able to if you're leaving," she added, sounding sadder and sadder as she spoke.

"Well, we can help while they're here," someone behind her said.

"Thank you all for your help. We don't have enough puppies to go around, but if eight of you want to help feed them now, that would be great."

"I'll go get their food," Tom offered before heading into the kitchen. "Be back in a few minutes."

"And you're welcome to help in whatever new location I find too. Besides that, I know they can use more volunteers at the animal shelter."

Eight volunteers separated themselves from the rest and went to stand by the doggy area.

"I'd like to buy some treats for my dog," one of the others left in the group said to Sue. "They freeze, don't they? I don't want to run out during the time you're moving to another location."

"They sure do," Sue assured her as she went back to the front counter. "Come pick out the ones you want."

The other customers milled around the store, and many selected treats and sweaters or new leashes to buy. By the time Tom returned with the bottles and bowls, most had lined up at the register with armfuls of products to buy. Sue waited on them while Terri and Tom handed the bowls and bottles to the volunteers who were going to feed the puppies.

Most sat on the chairs and bench that Terri had near the puppy cages while a couple sat cross-legged on the floor and leaned against the bench. Everyone, two-legged and four-legged alike, looked like they were enjoying themselves.

Later, when all the puppy tummies were full and their eyelids weighed down with sleep, Terri and Sue returned them to the blankets in their cages where they could sleep comfortably. They thanked all the volunteers again as they wished her success in her fight and left the shop.

"Did Blake really say to give up without a fight?" Sue asked as soon as she had a chance after they were gone.

Terri nodded. "But I'm going over to M&S after lunch and see if I can reason with them again. At least I can honestly say that I've been to an attorney who says I'm in the right. I'll just leave out the part about not being able to hire him. If I get the same stonewall treatment after that, I'll go see a realtor to start the hunt for a new place."

"I can't believe this is all happening," Tom

said as he piled the empty bowls and bottles on the baking sheet he used as a tray to take them back to the kitchen to wash. "Everything was going so well, and then *boom*."

"I know you're concerned about your jobs, and I'll do my best to get resituated right away," Terri promised. "I don't want you guys out of a job for any time at all if I can help it. But I understand completely that you both have to be realistic. I wouldn't blame you if you lined up something else right away. In a pinch I could do the baking and hire temporary clerks from an agency to cover the shop until I found new people after the move."

"You are the greatest boss a person could have," Sue said with her hands folded over her heart. "I'll stick it out as long as I can."

"Me too," Tom echoed with a grin. "Working here is fun and a lot less stressful than owning the place." His grin disappeared. "Oh, I guess you're the one bearing the stress, aren't you?"

Terri smiled and thanked them. "That's how it works. Well, I'll look at today's mail and then eat my sandwich. I'm not feeling hungry, but I wouldn't want my stomach to growl when I'm making my pitch at M&S," she said to try to lighten the mood. "Anyway, I think I'll go over to M&S at one-thirty to try and catch Mr. Snyder. I'm guessing he returns from lunch about then. Call me if you need me in the meantime. I'll be catching up on the mail orders in the office. That reminds me, I'll have to get new flyers with the new address once I find a place."

Before she started on the mail orders, Terri called her friend and neighbor Marty at the newspaper where she worked.

"Is it a problem to call you at work?" Terri asked.

"It's not if I don't stay on the phone too long."

"Well, I'll be quick. I just want to ask a question."

"Fire away," Marty replied.

"First let me say that the lawyer this morning told me it would cost a fortune to fight it so that if I can't get them to change their mind, I should start looking for a new store location."

"Oh, hon, I'm so sorry. I know how you love it there."

"And I'm not giving up. I was thinking of ways to get public opinion on my side. I certainly have a lot of customers. So I was wondering, if I thought of something to do to get the public's attention, would it be hard to get the paper to cover it — without costing me a lot, I mean?"

"Hey, they're always looking for events to feature. I don't think it would be hard." She laughed. "I'll even put in a good word for you, if a secretary-slash-budding reporter has any say. Just let me know when you figure it all out."

"Thanks, Marty. That's what I wanted to hear."

"Good, so I'll see you soon."

Terri ended the call and leaned back in her chair. There had to be something she could do without breaking the law to draw attention to the fact that they were kicking her out. She had to think of something to make the public like her in that location so much that they wouldn't let M&S make her leave.

That afternoon Sue watched as three women walked into K-Nine Treats and marched to the register, where she stood putting price tags on the latest batch of fresh treats Tom had baked in the kitchen out back. She couldn't tell if they were angry or just determined.

"Hi. Can I help you?" she said in her friendliest manner.

"Well," one of them said, looking at the

others for support, "is Terri in now?"

Sue shook her head. "No, she's not, but I expect her back soon. I don't think she expected her meeting would take long."

"Oh," said the woman who seemed to be the leader of the trio, looking at her friends, "I don't know if you remember us, but we come in to feed the puppies whenever we can, and we always get treats for our dogs here."

"We each got the yellow raincoat and the little boots too. We love the boots you carry because they really do stay on their feet," another interrupted her to put in.

Grinning, Sue said, "That's wonderful. There's not a problem with that, is there?"

"Oh, no, none at all," the woman replied. "We have no problem at all with your store, and that's why we're here."

Sue frowned. "Come again?"

"Let me tell her," the woman who had been silent so far said. "You see, we were here before, when Terri explained that she'd received an eviction notice, and we think that's terrible." She looked to the other two women, who nodded.

"We can't bear the thought of her having to move this wonderful shop away. We want to help keep her right here."

"That is terribly sweet of you," Sue told

them with a broad smile, "but I can't see how you can help."

The younger and more snappily dressed of the women stepped forward. "I think I do. You see, my husband has a small advertising agency here in town, and I help him."

She named the agency and Sue said she had heard of them. "But I don't think that placing more ads will make them take back the eviction notice," Sue put in. "Besides, if we do have to move, spending more money right now wouldn't be a good idea."

"No, no, I'm not here to sell you ads," the woman replied with a smile and a negative wave of her hand. "I talked to my husband about the predicament Terri is in. He thinks that if we had enough general public support from people who want you to stay here, the development company might have to change their minds about kicking you out." She smiled proudly and waited for her opinion to sink in.

Frowning, Sue replied, "Yeah, Terri was thinking that too. We've certainly had support from our regular customers, but how do we get the public in general to want to keep us here? Lots of people don't have dogs or even know that we're here. They don't know what we have to sell or what we do here."

"They will when we get done. We put our heads together and came up with an idea that will let the whole town know that you're here."

"But how could the whole town possibly learn of our predicament?" Sue asked.

"What you need to do is hold a pet parade," the woman said proudly.

"A pet parade?" Sue asked, frowning.

"We came up with the name too: Riverside's First Annual Halloween Pet Parade."

"That's a cute idea and timely with Halloween just over a month away, but how will that help?" Sue asked, still unclear as to what they were getting at.

The third woman stepped up and took over the explanation. "If you have the pet parade and offer prizes from the products you sell, we'll do our best to get everyone in town with a dog, or cat, or whatever, to dress them up in costume and come for the parade. You see, my husband works at the newspaper, and I know he can get the parade covered as news."

"That should certainly help," Sue replied. "People would at least know we were here if they read it in the paper."

"And he said he could write a story *each week* announcing that it was coming at Halloween time — whenever you hold it. He can tell everyone how popular your shop is by covering the story in each article from a different angle. I know he's going to want to write about rescuing abused puppies and caring for them here. You might even get some more volunteers out of it."

"Yes, he could write about someone sewing a special costume for their rescued pet," another of the trio put in.

"Or he could write about kids making their own costumes for their pets. Kids always make good stories in the feature section," the third said.

"We figure that the public would like the idea of your parade so much that they would want you to hold it again next year. The First Annual Parade would have to have other parades follow in future years. The development company wouldn't dare close you down if enough people want you here next year. They could write letters to the editor, and M&S wouldn't want the negative publicity."

The three women beamed as they waited for Sue's reaction. A smile gradually grew on her face as she slowly nodded. "The idea sounds like it just might work in our favor. With M&S just starting the Riverside Two addition, they've got to care about public opinion. Say, could you come back later this afternoon and tell Terri all about your idea?"

"Sure we can," the women chorused.

"We're going to Soup and Salad down the walkway for a late lunch," one said.

"We always come late so we don't have to wait in line," another added.

"If we came back after that, do you think she'd be here?" the first asked.

"I'm not sure. She's just gone over to M&S to see the lease agent again," Sue replied. "Maybe if you all had dessert with your lunch, she'd be back by then," she added with a laugh.

"That works for us," one woman said, sliding her hand over her ample hip. "We'll stop back then."

The trio walked out of the store and Sue ran to the back to talk to Tom about their idea before the next customer came in.

"Is Mr. Snyder in?" Terri asked of the receptionist at M&S.

The woman looked up at her and frowned. "Do you have an appointment?"

"Well, no, but I just wanted to talk with him for a few moments. Can't he fit me in?"

"I'm sorry, but without an appointment, you can't see him."

"He's tied up now?" Terri asked.

"Would you like to make an appointment?" the receptionist replied, totally ignoring her question.

Terri sighed. "Yes, if I need an appointment to see him, then I would like to make an appointment," she said without hiding her annoyance. "How about in five minutes if he's free?"

The receptionist flipped through several pages of the daily calendar on her desk and then consulted the screen on her computer.

"Well, he can see you next week. Let me see . . ."

"He's tied up all this week?" Terri asked. All she could think was that she was losing time and money with each day she had to wait. Waiting nearly a week or more to see him meant that she'd have much less time to find another location if they ended up going through with the eviction.

"How about next Tuesday? Shall we say at nine in the morning?"

Terri released a breath in a rush as her shoulders slumped in defeat. "Tuesday at nine it is, then. Thank you."

"Do you want me to write that down for you?"

"No, thank you. There is no way I could forget."

Terri turned on the ball of her foot and walked out of the office. She itched to turn down the hall and open Bob Snyder's door just to satisfy herself that he *was* with another client or out of the office, but of course she didn't. All she could do at this point was return to her shop to help Sue. The after-school bunch of kids that came in each weekday to play with the puppies required extra supervision.

Carter had come out of his office to walk down the hall to see Bob when he saw Terri at the receptionist's desk. Stopping in his tracks, he backed up and flattened against the wall, out of sight, in case she looked his way. Immediately, he felt foolish for having done so. This was his company and he should have no reason to hide from anyone. And yet he had, because he'd never gotten around to telling Terri that he was the *M* in M&S. He'd had every intention of telling her — he just hadn't done it yet, he rationalized to himself. And meeting her here like this wasn't how he wanted to tell her.

His mind raced to figure out why she was at M&S. She hadn't come to see him because he'd never told her that he worked there. But her shop was in Riverside, and he quickly decided that she must have some business here because of that.

As he listened to the conversation at the reception desk, he could tell she was annoyed at being put off. Wondering if the receptionist was acting on Bob's orders, he remembered that he'd never asked him about Terri. With the long hours he was putting in on the drawings for the next section of Riverside, he hadn't remembered to do it.

The conversation at the reception desk stopped, and he heard the swish of the glass entrance door closing. Terri was gone and he could quit acting like a schoolboy hiding out of sight to keep from getting into trouble. He turned his steps to Bob's office and walked in with a single knock. Bob was going over financial record books that were spread out on his desk.

"I thought you had all that on your computer," Carter remarked.

"Yup, I do. And when these, my backups on paper, don't match what the computer tells me, I have to figure out why."

"Now I know another reason I became an architect. I can let someone else punch numbers," Carter said with a laugh. "Hey, you just missed seeing a very pretty lady. Marge at the front desk turned her away until next week."

Bob stopped comparing columns and looked up then. "That's what I told her to do until I get these columns to match. I wonder who it was." Depressing the button on the intercom, he asked Marge who had been to see him.

"It was Ms. Terri Bookman," she replied.

"Thanks," Bob said before ending the connection. "Ah, so Ms. Bookman was here again — the problem that doesn't want to go away."

Startled at the idea that Terri could be a problem for anyone, Carter dropped into one of the chairs facing Bob's desk. He wanted to hear about the problem with Terri.

"How can a woman that pretty possibly be a problem?" he asked lightly.

"She's the one with the pet store that I thought was going to be a specialty bakery. Instead of filling the outdoor tables and chairs with people munching on her treats, she has a constant line of customers and their dogs waiting to buy dog bones they bake there on the premises."

"I don't get it. How can a constant line of customers be a problem?"

"Hey, whose side are you on?" Bob asked, looking up from where his pencil marked in place in the long column of numbers.

"Explain the problem to me. I'm interested," Carter said, not moving.

"Okay, the customers come with their

dogs. That means they can't visit any of the other stores because dogs are not allowed. Only some tie their dogs to a tree or sign and go on in the other shops. Then those shop owners feel the dogs sitting there are a danger to their other customers. In fact, I'm having signs painted to keep dogs off the walkway altogether. We have to allow them on the grass by the river, which is city property, but we can keep them off of the walkway by the shops."

"That sounds a bit extreme. And what are you doing about Ms. Bookman and her store?"

"We're evicting them," Bob said flatly as if it were obvious. "Nice guy that I am, I gave her an extra thirty days, but come the middle of November, she'll be history here. Then I get in a human-type bakery, and by the holidays, they'll be up and running and people will flock to them for Christmas cookies and all."

"That's what we had planned for there?" Carter asked hesitantly. He'd really had little to do with the selection of clients; he just designed the shop space to fit what they needed. He didn't remember talking about a bakery there. Outfitting the kitchen had come after the space was rented.

"Right, listen, is that all you came in here

149

for? I've got to get back to these numbers."

Carter straightened in his chair and took just a couple more minutes of Bob's time to get the answer to the question he'd originally planned to ask before he saw Terri out front.

As he walked back to his office, he could hardly believe it. Terri was being evicted from Riverside and, when she found out he owned half of it, she would probably blame him as much as Bob. And he didn't want that to happen. How would he ever tell her where he worked now?

But how could he continue to see her and not tell her?

Back in her office, Terri slipped out of her heels and stepped into her comfortable shop shoes. Sticking her head back into the kitchen to check the nearest feeding schedule, she found out she was just in time to help. She could count on feeding and cuddling the puppies to improve her spirits.

"I'll take the tray out. Thanks, Tom," she said, picking up the tray he had ready right on time.

Backing through the swinging door, she was startled to see the largest group of people yet that had apparently come to feed the puppies. The benches were full, and nearly a dozen more sat on the floor while several more stood nearby. The shop was literally full of people.

"There she is," one cried and all the conversation stopped.

She felt as if she were on stage as they watched her carry the puppy food and bottles to the dog crates.

"Wait until you hear what they have to say," Sue told her excitedly, a big grin on her face. "They all want to keep the shop here and they all want to help you make sure it does. Isn't that great?"

Terri stopped as volunteers, who had done it before, began to set out the bowls for the Labs. Holding the folded towels and bottles for the tiny ones, she looked around at all the eager faces. She couldn't help but smile. "What is it? What do you have to tell me?" she asked.

"Well, we've been talking about a plan that we think will save the shop. And we would all like to help you with it," a regular customer sitting on the bench said.

"Unless one of you is a magician, I don't see what we can do, but I'm sure willing to listen. Let's get these hungry guys fed first, though."

As Sue found the volunteers to feed the tiny ones, Terri handed them each a puppy on a folded towel and a bottle. After collecting the bowls from the Lab puppies that had finished eating and licked them clean already, she turned back to the group.

"Okay, now then, I'd love to hear your idea."

"It was my husband's and my idea, so I've been elected to tell you all about it. We think you should have the First Annual Riverside Halloween Pet Parade. We all know it will be so successful that people won't want you to leave so you can hold it again next year." She grinned. "M&S will have to let you stay. And here's how we think you should do it."

After the women left the store, Terri went to her office to think about their idea. She went over and over the plans, making improvements where she thought they would work better. She gathered Sue and Tom's ideas and thought some more. By closing time, she'd decided it was a good plan and just might work.

One thing was for sure: she wasn't about to cave in and move without trying her best to get M&S to let her store stay where it was.

CHAPTER SEVEN

Even with all that was happening during the week, Terri looked forward to dinner with Carter on Friday night. The fact that he was taking her to the restaurant that had supplied their delicious picnic was a bonus.

On Wednesday, she had what she knew would be a joyful reunion to attend. Tom helped her put the Lab puppies into the large cage in the back of her car. They seemed nervous about the unusual trip in the middle of the day and barked excitedly.

"They know something's up," Tom said. "Isn't it amazing? You put them in the car to go and come from the shop everyday, but they know this is different."

"Dogs are amazing on a lot of levels. Do you know that some dogs can tell if a person has certain kinds of cancer? Some countries use dogs regularly to spot the cases, and then they do the tests to confirm it. The dogs are correct over ninety percent of the time. Sometimes when the tests said there was no cancer after the dogs said there was, the patients contracted it later."

"Do you suppose the dog knew that before the doctors could prove it?"

Terri shrugged. "There you go, guys," she said, putting the last puppy inside. She reached beside the cage for the pair of knotted heavy socks that she kept there. "Here, you can play with these," she added, tossing them into the cage and shutting the door.

Tom shut the back hatch on the SUV. "How long before the little ones in the shop can go to good homes?"

"That's up to the 'powers that be,'" Terri told him. "They're coming along nicely, but it should be at least a week longer — maybe the first part of October. If it comes to moving the shop, it'll be good they're gone by then. I'll need the time to pack and get the new place ready." She frowned. "I guess I should call Sam and tell him I'm out of the running as a helper for a while."

"Or you can use the time to gear up for Christmas shoppers once the parade tells everyone you're here and makes them let you stay," Tom countered with a laugh.

"Thanks, I needed that. Positive thinking it is."

Sliding in behind the steering wheel, Terri

154

waved a good-bye to Tom, who was already returning to the back door of the shop. That door was so handy to the parking lot. It was really too bad that she wouldn't be around long enough to explore the possibilities of making the door an entrance for the customers there. Wouldn't it be fun if they could somehow see what Tom was cooking up in the kitchen on their way into the store? He could be quite entertaining, and she bet kids would love it.

The trip to the farm where the barn had burned took a little longer than it had on the night of the fire when few cars had been on the road. Eventually, she pulled into the farmyard and heard barking at once. She saw a Lab run from the corral straight to the car. Immediately, the little quartet in the rear answered her with barks.

Apparently, she had been brought home earlier than expected. Running all around the car then, she stopped at the back door and raised her front paws to the bumper so she could see in the back window. Inside, her puppies continued barking with enthusiasm.

The farmer followed the dog's path from the corral and his wife soon came out from the house. Terri expected the children to run out too, but they would be at school, she quickly realized.

Walking to the back of her car, Terri could see a large area on the dog's back where the hair was very short. The burns were healing nicely, but it would be some time until the hair grew back to cover the scars if ever.

"I'm so glad you're here. She came home this morning and she's been poking into every corner looking for her pups ever since."

"Then we won't make her wait another minute," Terri replied.

The farmer took her collar and pulled her back so Terri could open the hatch. The barking was incessant from all the dogs now. Terri opened the crate and took out one puppy. Holding her side against the door to prevent the others from jumping down and possibly hurting themselves, she lowered the puppy to the ground. When she'd released them all, they all ran around, happy as could be.

"I can't thank you enough," the farmer's wife said. "The rescue shelter says you and your customers volunteer your time and money to care for rescued animals whenever you're needed. We don't know what we would have done without help. If there's anything we can do to thank you, please let us know."

The parade plans that bounced around in her head came to the fore. Would it work? If the public liked what she did there, would M&S let her stay?

If she didn't try it, she'd never know. And she'd never been one to give up without trying.

"Actually, there is something that you and all these little guys can do to help."

"Well, why don't you come on in for a cup of coffee and tell us what it is?" the farmer's wife said to Terri. "You can take a break now too, can't you?" she asked her husband, who nodded. "Good," his wife said, leading the way to the kitchen door.

Terri latched the cage and lowered her car door and followed. When they sat around the kitchen table with mugs of hot coffee in their hands, Terri began to explain what she had in mind. "I'll try to make a long story short, but I'm being evicted from my shop and some very nice people are trying to help me get the company to let me stay there. I'd like to feature your dogs in a story about what we do there to see if that could help turn public opinion in our favor. Then letting me stay there would be in the owner's best interests too."

She took a deep breath. "And I'd like your dogs to lead the Halloween pet parade we're planning to start at the shop and go the length of Riverside on the path by the river."

From the smiles on their faces, Terri knew she had two new supporters. Explaining the particulars was easy then. "The parade will be the Saturday before Halloween," she continued.

As she waited for Carter to arrive to pick her up for dinner that Friday evening, Terri was both upset and cautiously optimistic. Each time she thought of being evicted, she still got angry because she was in the right but couldn't afford to take it to court. Then she would remember the plans for the parade and feel optimistic about her chances of building public opinion high enough to stay there. However, some moments she wanted to knock everyone who worked at M&S upside the head to see if that helped. But being basically a peaceful person, thinking about doing it didn't help her anymore than actually doing it would have done.

Ready to go out except for the addition of her dress instead of her dressing robe, she fed the puppies their bottles after a little puppy food softened with formula that she'd started feeding them after the Labs had gone home. Secretly, she hoped that adding more mushy puppy chow with formula tonight would keep them happy for a longer time while she and Carter were out. She and Carter would still come right back after dinner, but it would be nice to sit and enjoy a cup of coffee instead of changing out of her favorite dress to feed puppies again.

The puppies had taken to the solid food right off. She almost wished she had started it sooner, since it meant they went longer at night without interrupting her sleep. But the vet had told her to go easy and get them accustomed to getting the formula on a regular basis first. With the little balls of fur all asleep with full tummies, she returned to her bedroom and changed into her blue and black print dress with the calf-length skirt that swirled softly around her legs as she walked.

Adjusting a silver chain around her neck, she leaned forward closer to the mirror. Were those frown lines beginning between her eyebrows? Were they from all the worrying she'd been doing lately? She smoothed them with her fingers and checked her hair when the doorbell rang. He was a little early. She hoped that meant he was looking forward to the evening as much as she was — and not just for the good food.

Swinging the door open for him to enter,

she smiled as his gaze swept over her from the top of her head to her toes and back.

"Very nice," he said softly. Grinning suddenly, he added, "Yup, you clean up real nice."

Laughing, she punched his shoulder playfully and turned away to get her coat and purse. "Partial as I am to my sweats or jeans, I figured I'd give you a treat and let you see me in a skirt," she joked back. "I don't wear them often, so enjoy."

"I am," he said. "I am. In fact, I'm enjoying it so much that I'd kiss you if you hadn't already put on your lipstick. I'll have to come even earlier next time." Chuckling, he helped her into her coat. "Hey, it's quiet in here. The Labs are gone."

"Yes, they've enjoyed a happy reunion with their mother and the farm family. They said to thank you for your help."

He nodded. "How's their mother doing?"

"She'll heal, but it will take time, and her coat will never be the same. The pain will go away, which is the best part."

Terri grabbed her purse and said good-bye to the boys before she and Carter left the apartment. Driving to the restaurant, Terri found it hard to turn off thinking about her eviction. It affected every aspect of her life because it might completely cut off her livelihood. So how could she not think about it? Worriedly, she constantly rubbed the strap from her purse that lay on her lap.

"I can tell something's bothering you," Carter said softly, glancing in her direction. "I don't think that you've stopped frowning since we left your apartment. Are you using body language to tell me you're not enjoying going out with me?"

Quickly she smiled and looked at him. "Oh, no, it's not that at all." She raised her hand to smooth the wrinkles between her brows again. "You're very perceptive. There is something bothering me."

Arriving at the restaurant, she insisted on walking with him from the parking lot instead of letting him drop her off at the door. The hostess seated them in a booth in a row that was elevated a low step over the floor containing the tables and chairs so they could see the view of the falls beyond the bridge. On the end of the row and in a corner, their booth felt tucked away and private — a place they could talk without being overheard.

"I haven't quite made my way down the whole menu, but everything I've tasted here has been good," he said.

"You say you don't like to cook," she

proposed with a laugh.

"Haven't had time lately, but I'm not totally inept in the kitchen."

The waiter took their orders and left to get their beverages. Terri leaned back and surveyed the view. Though already dark out, there were enough city streetlights on to highlight the rushing water. Thinking how much she would miss seeing that view each day, she didn't realize how long she had been silent.

"Would it help to talk about it?" he asked softly.

"Oh, I'm sorry. I guess I do get lost in my problems more often than I like."

"Sharing may make the load lighter."

"Well, it's a long story. Are you sure you want to hear this?" she asked.

He shrugged. "I'd be glad to listen — that is, unless you'd rather talk about something else."

Meeting his gaze, she debated whether to tell him or not. But he was an architect, and he might be able to advise her. After leaving the shop that afternoon, she had formulated more definite ideas of how to make the shop workable with a rear entrance, and hopefully keep everyone happy by keeping dogs off the walkway. It didn't give M&S the people-type bakery they wanted, but it might be enough to change their minds. But did she want to impose on her new relationship with Carter to ask him his professional opinion? She didn't want him to feel used.

But with her time until the eviction running out fast, she had no choice. Feeling that she had to explore all avenues, she took a deep breath and began. "I'll try to make the long story as short as possible. You see, I'm being evicted from my shop at Riverside. I've talked to a lawyer and he says I could win the case if it went to court, but I would probably lose everything by the time I got a judgment and paid my attorney fees."

When the waiter brought their salads and interrupted her just then, she couldn't help but notice that Carter looked relieved. Maybe he really didn't want to get involved. She felt badly for having even started to involve him, but as long as she'd started . . .

Between bites of the fresh greens, she gave him an opportunity to tell her that he'd heard enough. "It's all very confusing. Have I made it as clear as mud?" she asked with a grin. If he wasn't interested in hearing more, then he could tell her now.

"Do you think the public support or refitting your shop entrance would make them change their minds?" he asked instead.

She laughed. "I wish I knew that." Her smile disappeared and she frowned again. "But I can't sit and do nothing. When I know I'm in the right, I fight. So I'm working on three fronts. One is to prove that my shop is very, very popular and nearly invaluable to Riverside. Then I hope M&S would have to let me stay. The second front of this battle for survival is to figure out an entrance that wouldn't impact the rest of Riverside."

After taking a sip of water, she set her glass down and smiled. "The third front is demanded by my practical side." She twisted her face comically in a look of disgust. "I've started to look at the paper for ads of other shop sites that are vacant. There are a lot that are available, which doesn't bode well for their locations or business in general. I mean, if it's such a good location, why did the previous business leave?"

He nodded.

Toying with the last of her salad, she sighed. "I keep thinking that if I could remove the objections to my shop, they might let me stay where I am."

A busboy interrupted the conversation by picking up their empty salad bowls and refilling their water glasses.

"You sound like you've thought it out carefully," Carter put in once they were alone again.

"I've tried to, but I would welcome advice from you about a new entrance," Terri replied, "if you don't mind giving me a little free architectural advice, that is."

He smiled, but for some reason Terri thought he also looked wary, even worried. Maybe he didn't like people to ask for free advice for which he would normally charge probably a good deal. She couldn't blame him for that. And she didn't want to put him on the spot. With no time to study her situation, how could he come up with an answer? She was expecting too much of him and probably shouldn't have brought it up at all. But then he had asked.

"What is it you want to know?"

He got a short reprieve when the waiter brought their entrées. They agreed they looked delicious and began eating.

"You were going to tell me . . . ?" he said to start her back in the conversation where she'd been.

"Well, I always come and go through the back door on the corner of the building that leads to the kitchen. Going out the front is a longer trip to the car, so the steps add up when I have to make multiple trips with

165

puppies."

She grinned. "I think putting a customer entrance there could really work. I was wondering if it would be feasible to put in a hall from the back door that passed by the kitchen and ended up in the shop. It would run along the outside wall somehow. The kitchen's not very big, but I'd sacrifice a few feet along that side in order to gain the new entrance."

Picturing the changes, she leaned back in her chair.

"Actually, I thought it would be neat to put a window from the new hall into the kitchen. People could watch the baker at work when they came in that way. It might be fun for kids to come and see what he does."

He nodded but didn't speak. Taking a deep breath, she went on with her explanation.

"Our customers could avoid the walkway in front of the shops altogether that way. There could be no more complaints of the dogs coming in and out of the shop bothering other shoppers out there."

Setting down her fork on her empty plate, she chewed the last bite and patted the corners of her mouth with her napkin. "But then if M&S were looking to us to be a magnet for the whole row of shops with a people-bakery, the new entrance wouldn't help. It wouldn't get our customers to go on down the walkway to shop elsewhere too. They would have to leave their dogs at home to do that."

"That's not unreasonable to expect, is it?" he asked guardedly. "I don't know a store, other than yours, that allows dogs to enter — other than medically necessary dogs."

"No, but many people bring their dogs in to try a coat or sweater on them before they buy it. So all it would do is avoid having dogs on the walkway — something I guess they are going to outlaw any day now when the signs are painted and put up."

"Are you finished, ma'am?"

Startled by the waiter's appearance at their table, she nodded. "Yes, thank you."

He took their plates and returned to ask if they wanted dessert. In those few minutes, Terri wondered why Carter hadn't said much beyond asking questions. She concluded that without knowing the building, he was having a problem visualizing what she was saying about the architectural changes. He'd probably never seen her shop and didn't understand about the back entrance idea at all. It wasn't as if he had been the architect who designed Riverside and knew all the shop spaces. Hoping for way too much from him, she had to let him off the hook.

"I shouldn't be dragging you into this, and just talking about it has my stomach doing flip-flops again. I think we should talk about something else, okay? I don't want to get an ulcer over this whole thing, and I sure don't want to spoil this lovely dinner for one second more."

Carter looked at the distressed look on Terri's face and felt his own stomach do flip-flops. He was stuck. As a half owner of M&S who had nothing to do with rentals, he couldn't void the eviction. But as a man who didn't want his relationship with Terri to end, he had to do something. As a man who had come to care for her more than he'd ever expected to, he wanted to make her happy. He wanted to see her smile again.

"You should have seen the Labs when I took them home," she said brightly. "Their mother was already there. They were all so happy and noisy. You should have seen them jumping all around."

Her smile filled her face and made her eyes sparkle. Yes, that was the smile he wished he could keep on her face. There had to be some way he could help, or just to help soften the blow — without telling her he had anything to do with the company that was evicting her. He would tell her eventually, of course, but not until the dust settled and he had helped her set up shop somewhere else.

And he would do his best to make the transition smooth for her. That might at least minimize any negative reaction when he told her that it was his company that had forced the move.

Terri brought two mugs of hot chocolate into her living room later that evening. As she passed Carter, who was squatting in the hall petting the little puppies, she smiled. The tykes sure did like the attention he was giving them. She only hoped they wouldn't put up a fuss and expect something to eat now when she'd rather sit quietly for a while with Carter.

Setting the mugs on coasters on the coffee table, she kicked off her heels and sat on the couch with one leg folded under her. That way she sat sideways and could face him when he sat next to her. She smoothed her skirt over her legs and reached for her mug.

"Dinner was really delicious," she offered.

He rose and came toward the couch. "I just stopped in the place on my way home

169

one night when I was too tired to even think about cooking, and I'm glad I did. I've never had a bad meal there."

As she watched over her mug, he sat beside her and sipped his drink. "Mmm, this is good."

He'd been strangely quiet and non-communicative as the evening had worn on. She wondered if something wasn't wrong with the new project he said he was working on. Even knowing him such a short time, she was optimistic he would work it out. In the meantime, she understood that he had a lot of extra work now on his mind. They both did. Now was not the easiest of times to begin a new relationship for either of them.

The puppies saved them from a strained conversation. They must have figured out that drinking hot chocolate was as good as eating, and they wanted in on the action too. Or at least they wanted more attention than they were getting with the two humans sitting across the room on the couch. Their insistent yips could no longer be ignored.

"I guess I should feed them," Terri said hesitantly. Though they each had their worries on their minds, she hoped he wouldn't take that as an excuse to leave. She didn't want the evening to end.

"Can I help?"

She laughed. "Not in those good clothes you can't. I have to change too before I get near them. I'm not sure that a dry cleaners could get out puppy stains."

Swallowing the last of his sweet drink, he set the cup down. Night and Day rose from lying at their feet and nosed in the cup, licking the rim.

"Oh, no you don't. Chocolate's not good for you," Terri told them as she picked up the mug and carried it to the kitchen with her own.

Behind her, she heard Carter following. At the sink, she rinsed out the mugs and turned to face him. He leaned his hands on the edge of the counter on each side of her. "If I can't help, then I should at least get out of your way."

Her disappointment was great enough to feel like a heavy cloak draped on her shoulders. "Thank you again for dinner," she said. "And thank you for listening to my problems. I shouldn't have burdened you with them, but actually it was good to explain the situation to someone again. Each time I do, I try to think of something else I can do in order to stay in the shop where I am. I've been so happy there."

Embarrassed at bringing up her problems

again, she turned away. Raising his hand, he turned her face back to him and ran his knuckles along her jaw. "I hate to see you upset."

"Well, I'll be fine when it's all settled — though if I can't relocate, I can't imagine doing anything else like working in an office. I couldn't keep my dogs." She groaned and looked to the ceiling. "Here I go again. Anyway, thanks for listening." She rose onto her toes and kissed his cheek. "You're a very sweet man. Do you know that?"

"And you're going to send this sweet man home in favor of feeding dogs?"

"The next time you want to wear that suit, you'll thank me," she said with a laugh.

Wrapping his long fingers around the back of her neck, he drew her face closer and kissed her. Impatient with the people standing there kissing instead of getting their formula out of the refrigerator to mix with the puppy food, the puppies objected energetically.

Curling her hands around his upper arms, she said, "Much as I'd like you to stay, I think you should go before I get evicted from here too, because of the noise. Come on — I'll walk you to the door," she offered with a grin.

The puppies jumped and yipped louder as

they passed the plastic pool.

"Shush. Give me a break, guys. I'll only be a few minutes more," she told them.

At the door he turned to her and cradled her jaw with one hand. Kissing her firmly, he said, "I wish I had a magic wand to wave in order to solve your problem, but I don't. There's really nothing I can do."

She laughed. "I know, and you have your own work to finish. I hope you solve the project you're stewing over too."

"I'm that obvious too, huh?"

"Yeah, you are. Is it serious?"

He shrugged. "The more time I spend on the problem, the more important it becomes to me. I'm not giving up until it's solved, but I just don't know how to solve it yet."

Terri grinned. "I can sure relate to that. I'd never believe you a quitter. You'll figure out something. We both will."

"In the meantime, I believe hugs go a long way to helping people who have problems to solve," she told him, raising her arms to around his neck. "At least it makes me feel better."

"That I can do," he said, drawing her to him. "You just let me know anytime I can help in that department," he offered, sliding his hands over the soft fabric of the back of her dress.

"Me too," she said with a smile as she looked up at him.

His kiss was firm before it softened to sweet nibbles that left her nerve endings singing. She didn't want him to stop. When they separated moments later, he looked at her with his frown back in place. Slowly, he dropped his arms and hers fell to her sides. As he reached for the door handle, he wished her a good night. Pausing longer, he looked at her so strangely that she wondered what he wanted to say.

A chill skittered down her back as he closed the door after himself without saying anything.

CHAPTER EIGHT

Sunday began with Terri's usual jog around the park with the boys. They all needed the exercise, but she hoped to see Carter too. She kept an eye out, but he and Fred never appeared.

The night before, she'd tossed and turned and hadn't been able to get much sleep. The remainder of the day dragged by with the hours spent in her usual weekend fashion when she wasn't at the shop — cleaning her apartment, washing her clothes, plus, of course, feeding, walking, and playing with the puppies.

While they ate, her practical side rose to control her, or was it that her worry over her predicament with the shop had gotten the best of her? Searching the classified ads in the paper, she circled the ones that sounded anywhere near right for a new shop location. She would call a realtor in the morning and see how soon she could make an appointment to see them all and any others the realtor would recommend.

Growing stronger and bigger every day, the puppies wanted attention more of the time and didn't sleep as long as before. Happily for her, however, they went longer between feedings. It wouldn't be long before they were down to just morning and evening. Playing with them was always a delight and calmed her. She couldn't help but get attached to the little darlings even though she knew the time was nearing when they would leave her.

If they were still her responsibility Halloween week, she decided to put them in the parade too. "How about the three little bears, and I could be Goldilocks?" she asked them as they played on the kitchen floor. "Or what about the three blind mice?" No, she thought. She'd never get dark glasses to stay on their heads.

Imagining what other trios the puppies could be kept her mind busy throughout her evening walk with the boys. As she lay in bed later, the distraction didn't work any longer. She'd thought of all the trios she could imagine, but her thoughts wandered back to her dilemma at the shop. She thought of the simple changes that would keep dogs off the walkway at Riverside, picturing an image of the back entrance and new hallway to her shop. The more she thought about it, the more she liked the idea, and the more she thought it just might work.

Carter had told her he wished he had a magic wand to help, but he didn't. She would try again with her appointment Tuesday morning at M&S — although, if Carter weren't so busy with his own work as an architect, she might have asked if he could come up with some simple drawings for her to take to show Bob Snyder at M&S at that meeting.

But that wasn't going to happen. Carter had enough on his mind and worked long hours on his own projects. Instead, she would look for her copy of the floor plan that M&S had given her to look at when she was considering renting the space. Unable to remember giving it back, she hoped it would be in her files. She could have a copy made and draw in the addition herself. It wouldn't have all the accurate detail an architect would put on the page, but she could certainly draw a straight line to scale. Then it would show Bob how easy it would be to make the changes and meet both their expectations.

Well, at least it would meet most of them.

She wasn't interested in opening a bakery for people. No, she had to make her pet bakery just as attractive to M&S as a people-bakery.

Still thinking about having a plan in place, she finally fell asleep.

For Carter, Sunday came and went in a flash. He wasn't cleaning or feeding dogs, but he was studying the blueprints for Terri's shop to see if an entrance at the side or back would work to keep the dogs off the walkway. More than a little surprised, he decided the entrance at the back with the new hall along the side as Terri had described would work just fine and at little added expense. It didn't have to change the footprint of the building at all. He liked the idea of putting in a window to the kitchen for people to watch the baker. The present window on the outside wall would provide natural light for the hallway too.

"But what about parking?" he mumbled to himself. Would there be enough in the area outside that door? And an entrance door would have to be put in that was to code.

Looking again at the plans for the landscaping and parking, he saw that there was room for parking. Of course, he could never designate those spaces for just her shop, but shoppers heading for the walkway in front of the shops would be more likely to take a space closer to where they were headed. He guessed they would be available to her customers most of the time.

Monday morning at the office, with Fred comfortable in his bed under the window behind him, he put the changes down on paper. He even worked up an estimate of what it would all cost to add the internal wall and new door plus the window to the kitchen. That afternoon, with the idea firmly in his mind and the completed drawings on his slant-top drawing table, he reached for the phone on his desk. "Marge, is Bob in?"

"Yes, sir, but he's with a client, and when he's done, he's leaving for his appointment at the bank. He said he was going right home from there instead of coming back here. He's got the workmen coming who will install new tile in his house tomorrow, and he wants to make sure they do it right."

"Oh, sure, I knew that. Um, I have something I need about fifteen minutes to talk to him about. Does he have any time tomorrow morning?"

He heard the receptionist flipping the page on her calendar. "Yes, his appointments start at nine. He's always in earlier than

179

that, so you could catch him before then."

"Good, I'll be there just after eight forty-five and clear out when his nine o'clock appointment shows up. Thanks."

Smiling at the prospect of solving Terri's dilemma and doing it in a way that was good for M&S, Carter sketched a rough elevation drawing of Terri's shop from the rear with the new entrance shown in the floor plan he'd finished. That completed, he rolled that up with the rest and cleared his drawing table. He had to get back to work on the new section floor plans. While the shops were laid out, he hadn't done much on the apartment building that would anchor one end. His deadlines were coming at him fast and furiously.

Having done the extra work on the project for Terri tightened his time constraints, but he wasn't about to stop wanting to help her. He wanted to believe he could convince Bob to go along with the changes and let her stay. Surely one of the restaurants already in Riverside could add a case of portable goodies that people could buy and eat at the tables in good weather. Frankly, he wasn't sure why Bob was so stuck on that idea. The main restaurant was already dealing with the city to get permission to have tables outside. By installing big propane heaters, their outdoor space under an extension of the roof could be used three seasons out of four. He hadn't heard if they had succeeded in getting the permit. He'd have to check.

"Stop," Carter ordered himself, running his hand through his hair and slapping his palm down on the drawing table. "Think Riverside Two!"

After working the rest of the day and long into the evening hours after quitting time, he even took some work home with him to double-check that evening.

By 8:00 the next morning, he'd finished an early jog with Fred and was back at work at the office. Bob, however, had a flat tire on the way to the office and didn't make it in until 8:35. Marge rang Carter's intercom when Bob arrived, as he'd asked her to do, and he went right down to his office. He wanted to finish their discussion before his 9:00 appointment came in.

"I've solved your problem with the eviction you served on K-Nine Treats," Carter said without preamble.

Laying out his floor plan and elevation sketch for Terri's shop's new rear entrance on Bob's desk, Carter looked over his shoulder and explained how easy the modifications would be. "The shop is located on the end of the row, so this would be easy to add," Carter explained. "It would get all the dogs going into her shop and off the walkway."

His partner looked over the drawings. "What's all this about? A wall costs money," Bob insisted. "What we need is a new tenant in there to make us money instead of keeping this one to cost us more."

"It wouldn't cost much, and it would solve the problem without any lawyers that do cost us money. Customers with dogs could enter in the rear, though what you have against dogs isn't clear to me. I've never heard of there being a problem with them at Riverside. Out of curiosity, who are the shop owners who object to dogs there?"

"Pierre doesn't like them," Bob replied offhandedly, still studying the large sheets of paper.

"Excuse me? That was singular — one renter's name. Is the eviction and all the fuss about dogs for the benefit of one shop, or in this case, one restaurant owner?"

"Hey, he pays rent on the largest space at Riverside. He says the dogs get into his garbage and people leave others tied to trees outside his front door. They bark and watch his customers eat, which makes them uncomfortable."

"Wait a minute. These are two different

problems here. His garbage is out back on the parking lot side. If dogs are getting into it there, they're loose and running around, and the restaurant's containers aren't what they should be. Call the dogcatcher and tell him he should use more secure containers. That's his problem, not K-Nine Treats' problem."

"I don't know. I just don't like dogs around there in general," Bob put in.

"And the dogs tied to the trees out front — are the owners in his restaurant?"

Bob shrugged. "They probably are."

"And does Pierre want the customers to leave?"

"Of course not. He just doesn't want the dogs there."

Carter was getting a bad feeling that this was a problem that had been blown all out of proportion. "Has anyone else complained about K-Nine's customers and their dogs?"

"No, I guess not. And I'm big enough to admit that I've heard some good things about the pet shop."

"It's not a pet shop. They don't sell pets. They sell food and accessories for pets." He straightened and looked directly at Bob. "Have you ever been in there?"

Bob shook his head. "No, have you?"

Taken back for a moment, Carter realized

he hadn't ever been in there since it had opened either. How had he missed getting the freshly baked treats for Fred?

"They have puppies in there and stuff for sale. How is that not a pet store?"

"The puppies in there have been rescued and are not for sale," Carter explained. "The owner helps the county animal shelter when they're overloaded. She and the customers feed them and play with them to socialize them so they'll make good pets. The animal shelter takes care of finding them good homes once they're old enough."

"That would explain why she doesn't have the licenses necessary to sell pets, I guess. I thought I could get her on that. But your solution here," he said, pointing to the drawings, "doesn't get us the specialty bakery that I thought we were getting in the first place."

"I vaguely remember talking about getting a bakery in the row somewhere, but the success of Riverside doesn't hang on getting one, does it? People can buy take-out desserts at any of the restaurants down there, and one of the smaller ones would probably put in a case of take-out food if you encouraged them to do that. Or you could put the bakery in the new section next year."

"I know, I know. Listen, Carter. I don't

know why you're involved in this or why you spent the time we haven't got on these drawings. We've already served the eviction notice. If I go back on that now, it will compromise my position in the eyes of the other renters for future dealings. I can't do that. And the same goes for the new entrance. If we add on for one, they'll all want something changed or built on."

"But this solution is so simple, and the owner likes it."

Frowning, Bob leaned back in his chair and looked up at Carter. "You've talked to her?" he asked incredulously. "Are you pulling an end run on me instead of sticking to our bargain of splitting the responsibilities here?"

"It's a long story, but I happen to know her. She told me about the eviction and her ideas for the new entrance." He shrugged. "It didn't take long to draw it up."

Bob glared at Carter. "Well, it ain't gonna happen. I'm not going to put out anything but a strong front when dealing with the shop owners. Anything else would mean trouble."

Carter looked at his watch. "Your nine o'clock is due any second. Look, we don't want bad relations with our renters. This woman has a lot of customers who want her to stay. Will you consider these simple changes before this goes any farther? I'd hate to see this in the newspaper."

"Okay, okay, I'll think about it and we'll talk again, but get these out of here for now."

Carter gathered up the drawings. "I'll leave these on the table by my window so you can come in anytime and look at them. And I'll be there all day if you have questions."

"Right." The intercom buzzed and Bob flipped the switch down. "Yes, Marge?"

"Your nine o'clock is here."

"Thank you. Send her on down."

"I'll get out of here," Carter said, rolling up the drawings and heading for the door where he turned back to Bob. "You'll talk to me later today?"

Bob waved his hand in a motion of dismissal. "Yes, I'll talk with you — if you'll admit why you're so all-fired interested."

Carter laughed and turned down the hall where Bob's nine o'clock would be coming toward him. When he looked up, he stopped dead on the spot. "Terri, what are you doing here?"

"What am I doing here? I have a nine o'clock appointment with Mr. Snyder to try again to talk him out of evicting me. But the more important question is, what are you doing here?"

Bob entered the hall from his office just a few feet behind Carter. Hearing her question, Bob laughed. "It sounds as if you two know each other but have never been properly introduced. Ms. Bookman, allow me to present Carter Morris, the M in M&S Development Company and the chief architect of Riverside."

Carter watched the blood leave Terri's face. She swallowed hard. "During all the time you knew about my eviction, you didn't tell me who you are. And when I tried to explain at dinner that I was fighting being evicted, I thought you might offer your opinion of my plan to solve the problem. Well, now I certainly know why you said nothing."

"Now, Terri, you don't know . . ."

"Don't you 'now Terri' me, you two-faced so-and-so. You . . . you must have been laughing into your napkin during my whole explanation at dinner." She closed her eyes and tipped her head up, fighting for control.

"No, Terri, that's not how it was at all." He reached to touch her arm, but she jerked it away. Her eyes sparkled. Was it with anger or unshed tears? Whatever it was, a few blinks later, the sparkle was gone.

"I thought we had something special

between us, Carter, but mister, you sure had me fooled. All you business landlords must have a club because the ones I've had both lie and pretend to be something they are not." She shook her head. "How wrong could I be about someone?" she asked, her voice strained and soft.

"Terri, I never got the chance to tell you I was with M&S. I didn't . . ."

Holding up her hand like a school crossing guard stopping traffic, she interrupted. "Please don't bother. I know how busy you are with your plans for the new addition to Riverside. That's your big project that's taking all your time, isn't it? Well, you certainly don't have to worry about me taking up any of your time in the future, Mr. Morris." She turned but paused. "Have a good day — both of you," she added with a smile that looked no more sincere than if it had been cut from construction paper and pasted on her face.

She walked down the hall when Bob's young assistant, the one who had served the eviction papers, stepped into the hall and blocked her path. "Oh, did she come to argue with you? I want you to know I made it very clear at her store that she had to be out in thirty days."

"No, I don't," Terri told him.

"No, she doesn't," Bob barked at the same time. "She has sixty days. I gave her thirty more."

"Nobody told me," the young man complained. "I thought evictions were all in thirty days."

"Go back to work," Carter told him sharply. "We'll handle this."

"If anyone is handling this, it will be me," Bob insisted, glaring at Carter and then his assistant. "Go back to work," he reiterated to his assistant, who hadn't moved. Looking bewildered, the young man backed up into his office and closed the door.

"Sorry, but you can't handle this," Terri said in a firmer voice to Carter. "Neither of you can," she added with a glance at Bob.

Some of the color had come back to her cheeks and Carter was glad of that.

"I have nothing further to say except that I have no intention of leaving my space at Riverside. I've talked to a lawyer and he says I'm in the right here. You have no legal reason to evict me. Believe me, I'm going to fight you with everything I've got. I have never deceived you, Mr. Snyder, and I can easily prove that. Not only that, but my customers want me to stay there. By the time the middle of November comes around, I will have public opinion so completely on my side that the public won't let you kick me out."

She turned to face Carter. "And to think that I believed that a dog lover could never be two-faced." Breathing rapidly, she strode down the hall and across the reception area.

"Terri, wait. Let me explain," Carter insisted. "You don't understand . . ."

She stopped at the door and turned back to him. "No, you have nothing to explain to me, Mr. Morris, Chief Architect and Co-owner of M&S Development Company. You have gotten all the information — or anything else — out of me that you are going to get. You want to talk? You can talk to my attorney. Good day!"

Two seconds later Carter was staring at the glass entrance door as it swung shut after Terri had marched out of the reception area. Feeling Marge's inquisitive gaze on his back, he strode back to his office without a word. Bob, who followed him, appeared in the door before he was even seated at his desk.

"I take it that the drawings you showed me this morning weren't because you had strolled past the shop and thought a new entrance would work better," Bob said.

"I never could put anything over on you, could I?" Carter asked just as sarcastically.

"Nope, but why do I seem to think you tried to put one over on her by not telling her who you are?"

"I don't suppose you'd believe me if I said I never intended to deceive her. The subject of where I worked never came up." He ran his hand through his hair and slapped it down on his desk. "What a mess this is. I finally find a woman I think I could really care for in a big way, and look what happens. She never wants to see me again."

"Yeah, well, since I have the next part of the morning free now, I'll spend the time going over those drawings. If she is going to fight this, maybe we should start looking for a compromise. I don't want the bankers to get wind of any lawsuit being brought against us now just when we're dealing with them on Riverside Two. The timing couldn't be worse for us."

Carter picked up the roll of drawings that he had dropped on his desk. "Have at 'em," he said gruffly. "And do let me know if you come up with a way to salvage my relationship with her, while you're at it."

His partner picked up the long roll and walked to the door where he stopped and turned back toward the desk. "You were right about one thing, buddy."

"I was? And what might that one thing

be?" he snapped.

"She is pretty."

Carter groaned and dropped his head into his hands. His friendship with Bob was strong enough to survive this, but he had to figure out something he could do to save his relationship with Terri — work deadlines or no deadlines.

With two significant losses — her shop and Carter — made so clear and so final, Terri reacted to the blows the only way she knew how. She stiffened her backbone and by the time she got back to the shop, she was ready for a fight — a fight to keep her shop, that is, not a fight to keep Carter. Sadly, she didn't feel she could ever trust him again after he'd deceived her and made a fool of her. She would, nonetheless, fight the eviction with every avenue she could find open — as long as it didn't cost her much money. Practical and realistic to the end, she knew she had to save that for moving in case it all did not work.

Marching into the shop with a quick greeting for Tom plus a promise to tell him all of what happened in a few minutes, she skirted around the cooling racks in the kitchen and headed right to her office. She'd stopped on her way to M&S to unload the dogs, and the boys came into her office from the shop run to greet her. She calmed herself considerably by petting them as she locked her purse in a desk drawer and stepped into her shop shoes. Reaching for the phone, she punched in Marty's cell phone number.

"Hi, it's Terri," she said when Marty answered right away. "I'll talk to you more at home, but my eviction stands. Anything you can find out about a features story on me would be really appreciated."

"Hey, I sure will. I love a good fight."

"Great, I'll talk to you about it some more this evening."

Ending the call and ready to do battle, she went out to help Sue open up.

"Aren't you going to change to work out here?" Sue asked, eyeing her smart gray suit and striped silk blouse that she'd worn to see Mr. Snyder.

"Thought I'd add a little class on a dreary Tuesday morning," Terri said, trying to jest with a smile. "But don't worry. Now that the puppies are eating from bowls instead of bottles, I stand a much better chance of not getting soiled. I just won't be able to sit on the floor and play with them."

"Well, we never are short of people who want to do that."

When they finished with the customer who had been waiting outside, Terri asked Tom to come out for a couple of minutes.

"From the fact that you're back already, and from the way you charged in here, I can guess what happened at M&S," Sue said when he arrived.

"And you'd be right. Not only is the eviction still on, but . . . but I discovered that Carter works there." She swallowed past the lump in her throat. "He's their architect."

"What? Your Carter works for M&S?"

She nodded. "In fact, he's the M in M&S, but he's definitely not my Carter."

"But that doesn't sound like the Carter you described, not the Carter who always made you so happy."

"Is this the Carter who helped you rescue the Lab puppies in the middle of the night?" Tom asked, trying to understand.

"He must be a master of disguises," Terri admitted.

"I guess so, and I'm sorry." Sue shook her head. "Oh, here's something for you." Sue handed Terri a phone message. "Sam called just before you got here after getting no answer at your apartment. He hoped he'd catch you before you left for work."

"Are there more puppies to be rescued?" Terri asked, brightening at the thought, but then realizing she shouldn't now, not when her future was so up in the air.

"No, he just asked about those little guys," Sue replied, pointing to the puppies. "I told him they were doing great and that they were weaned from the bottles."

"I suppose he's starting to look for good homes for them, then."

"When will they leave us?" Sue asked. "They are so cute that I want to keep them all."

"Me too," Terri said with a smile that felt good after a rotten morning. "I'd guess it'll be another week or two — whenever the vet gives the go-ahead."

"If you went ahead with the Halloween parade, wouldn't it be cute if they led the parade?" Sue asked.

"If you got Sam to walk with them, that could mean good publicity for Animal Rescue," Tom put in.

Terri smiled. "That's a good idea. He might take the time to do it — especially if it might net him some more volunteers."

"Then, you've thought more about the parade?"

Terri nodded. "It's a go! I even asked the owners of the Labs to be in it. They'll be good ads for service animals."

Sue clapped her hands and Tom laughed.

"Great," they agreed.

"Do you think those women who wanted to help will really follow through on it? I'd hate to go out with a monumental flop."

"They are in here so regularly to feed the puppies or just to play with them that I'm sure of it. They're full of good ideas and, I believe, good follow-through," Sue responded.

Terri took a deep breath. "Then let's do it up as big as we can!"

Sue let out a loud "Yahoo — the First Annual K-Nine Treats Halloween Pet Parade is on!"

"What can I do to help?" Tom asked.

"Well, let's get those women in here who are willing to help and figure out everything that has to be done to get all that publicity that will save us. My neighbor works at the paper and she wants to help too."

"Say, do you think that we'll have to have permission from M&S to have the parade?" Sue asked.

Terri laughed at the idea of having to ask them. "We are definitely not doing that. We don't want them to know what is going on until it happens." Gasping, she slapped her hand over her mouth and frowned. "Oh, no. I told Carter about the idea at dinner Friday."

"He wouldn't stop you, would he? The man can't be that big of a heel."

Though still wanting deep down to believe Carter would support her efforts, she shrugged. "I don't know. Carter's not the man I thought he was. There's no telling what he'll do, but we have to get this all organized and hit the paper with the entry form and initial story. Then I'd say they'd have a hard time stopping it."

"That's especially true since we'll be on public property on the walk by the river."

"That's right," Terri agreed.

"Listen, I'm sorry about Carter," Tom put in hesitantly.

Terri looked from him to Sue and then shook her head.

"It's just that, aside from the eviction, you've been so happy lately since you started seeing him. We were happy for you," Tom explained.

"Thanks, guys. I'm sorry it's over with Carter too." She sighed. "Okay, we're moving upward and onward now. Do you have the list of women who wanted to help?"

Sue pulled out a list from the shelf under the register and handed it to Terri as another customer came in. "Here you go."

"I'll go call them from my office. If we're lucky they can all get together tomorrow before we open so we can get this ball rolling. You two should make a list of any ideas you have, and I'll pay you for another hour to come in early tomorrow for the meeting if you can at such short notice." Both her employees assured her they would be there at 9:00 in the morning before they turned back to their regular duties.

Terri took the list to her office and sat at her desk. Each volunteer had put her name, address, phone, and e-mail addy on the list, so contacting them all would be easy. By the time she had explained her decision to each one, she had promises from all of them to come the following morning for the meeting.

The one whose husband worked for the newspaper was even going to bring him along to get the information for the sign-up form that would be published with the human-interest story that Saturday.

The fight had begun. But instead of a caring couple, she and Carter were adversaries.

CHAPTER NINE

Terri picked up her newspaper from the box by her mailbox after her jog with the boys on Saturday morning. She spread it out on the kitchen table and saw it at once. The story about K-Nine Treats' First Annual Costumed-Pet Parade on the Saturday before Halloween was the lead story in the features section.

"Yes," she cried, her fisted hand slicing down through the air. The boys got so excited at her outburst that she had to take a couple of minutes to pet them and assure them that all was well.

Going back to the article, she read that the parade would begin on the lawn in front of K-Nine Treats and would continue along the walk by the river. She'd gotten permission to hold the parade from the city. There was no way M&S could stop her now.

The story didn't mention that she was being evicted. That information would appear next week so they could build interest in the parade first and then show that it and the shop were threatened. She knew the reporter was going to call M&S to get a quote, and she had to wonder if they would consent to the interview. She could easily imagine Bob Snyder hanging up on him.

The blank form was in the lower corner where it could be easily cut out, filled out, and brought into the store to register an entry. She'd bought a sturdy, bright red plastic basket just the right size to contain them all so none would be misplaced. She'd put it on the checkout counter where entrants could see it and drop in their forms.

"Well, M&S, here we come," she said out loud. "If this works I won't be the only one objecting to the eviction."

Though excited with the possibilities, she turned to the back of the paper and found the realty section of the classifieds — business rentals. Scanning them, she found they were about the same list as the last time she'd looked.

She sighed. She hadn't had time to drive by any of them yet, and she hadn't contacted a realtor despite intending to. In fact, that was high on her to-do list, but so far she'd managed to avoid it. She had been very busy planning the parade, she rationalized. Truth be told, she didn't want to do anything that would signal in any way that she was giving up.

Night and Day walked to stand on each side of where she sat. They put their chins on her thighs, asking for some attention. She petted them each, scratching their ears the way they liked so much.

"Are you guys telling me I have to get going on finding another place?" she asked them. "I know. I know," she said as if they had replied verbally. "The attorney said the good guy doesn't always win, so I have to have another place lined up in case the eviction goes through."

She rose and headed for the coat closet. "Come on. The pups are asleep, so let's go get doughnuts and see if Marty is awake yet."

Night and Day didn't have to be told twice. They waited for her to fasten their leashes to the back of their harnesses and they were out the door ahead of her the moment she opened it.

"Next week," she told them as they crossed the parking lot. "I'll start looking at new shop locations next week."

The phone woke Terri late the next night. She'd fallen asleep on the couch while watching a bad movie on television. Thinking first that it might be Sam, she reached for the phone and said "hello" as brightly as she could.

"Hi, I hope it's not too late to call you."

"Is that you, Carter?"

"Yeah, it's me. Were you expecting it to be someone else?"

"I . . . I thought it might be Sam about another rescue."

"Oh, of course you'd think that at this time of night. Please don't hang up because it's me, Terri."

"What do you want, Carter?"

"How are the three little bundles of fur that you already have doing?"

"They're fine. Listen, Carter. I know you didn't call to talk about the puppies. As far as I'm concerned, you have nothing to talk about that I'd be interested in hearing."

"Terri, please listen to what I have to say. I've been working on a plan since our dinner together. . . ."

"Carter, I'm not interested in your plans. Whatever they are, they shouldn't include me anymore." Her breath caught and she had to swallow the lump rising in her throat. "I thought what we had was good, but I was wrong. It's over."

"Terri, no, it can't be. . . ."

"Please don't call me again."

She settled the phone back into the cradle even though she heard him still talking. Determined to not think about Carter and the hope she'd had for their relationship, she lay back down on the couch.

The boys jumped up and made themselves comfortable along the edge of the cushions in front of her. Petting them, she tried to watch the tube again to get caught up on the awful movie.

But she couldn't. The tears in her eyes made watching anything impossible. She cared for Carter so much, and she would never see him again.

Carter jogged in the park with Fred every day the following week and never saw Terri. He wondered if she had given up jogging so she wouldn't have to run into him. Her shop didn't open until way later than he had to be at work, so there was no reason for her to be out so early, he hopefully told himself. Waking to feed the puppies on demand had to be tiring, and it was good if she was getting extra sleep.

He, on the other hand, had no choice but to be at work early and stay late. The deadline for the blueprints and a three-dimensional model of the next section of

Riverside was November first. That was the target date he and Bob had set to have everything ready to go, to start the ball rolling on the loans from investors and the bank.

After jogging early, Carter had an extra hour of time at his desk by the window in his apartment, but he wasn't working on Riverside Two there. By spending time at home each morning for the past week, he'd completed the final floor plans and elevations to use to convince Bob to add a rear entrance to K-Nine Treats and to allow Terri to stay. Stopping to have them copied on his way to Bob's office, he arrived with everything ready including the accurately estimated costs for the whole project.

"I finished them for you," Carter said as he entered the office and approached the desk without even stopping first to take off his coat.

Instead of making room on his desk for the blueprints, Bob had spread out a sheet of newspaper to which he pointed. "Have you seen this? What's she trying to do?"

Carter set the rolls of drawings on the end of the desk and leaned over to see the story in point. "First Annual Costumed-Pet Parade for Halloween," he read out loud.

"Oh, yeah, she mentioned something about that."

"She mentioned it and you said nothing to warn me? Here I am trying to keep dogs off the walkway, and she's advertising to get dozens more."

Carter frowned. "Dozens — you really think that many will come?"

"Who knows?" Bob shrugged. "Any more is too many more."

"Hey, look at this as good exposure of Riverside to the public. Oh, look at this. It says they'll parade along the walk next to the river. That's public property and technically not part of Riverside. Only the city could keep her off that."

"And they can't because she went through all the right channels and got the permits. I called to find out."

Carter shrugged.

"I don't like this."

"Your kids don't have a dog you could enter?" Carter asked with a suppressed laugh.

"No, and you know it. I'm allergic to the smelly things."

"Aha, now I am beginning to understand. Allergies are why you don't like dogs and don't want them around," Carter concluded.

Pulling back his sleeve, Bob pointed to scars on both the top and bottom of one arm. "See these? A big dog did that when I was nine. It came at me out of nowhere when I was minding my own business walking home from school. I've hated the horrid creatures ever since."

"I'm sure someone has told you that you can't hate every dog because of what one did a lot of years ago."

"I don't hate all dogs, just ones I don't know. I like Fred. I don't keep you from bringing him to work, do I? Oh, and I like the cocker spaniel that my sister has because I know she would never bite me."

"What, your sister would never bite you?" Carter asked with a laugh. "Are you really sure of that — like even if you got her totally riled?"

Bob just glared at him.

"Well, two that you don't hate out of millions is a start," he said.

His partner crumpled up the newspaper and tossed it into the wastebasket. "Can't we stop this woman? I feel like I'm losing control here."

"If you fight this further you might as well tell the public that one of the owners of Riverside hates dogs and doesn't want them anywhere near his special shopping area."

Carter sat on the edge of the desk and looked up. "I can see the headlines now. The next thing they'll report about you is that you kick dogs each morning for exercise."

"Stop, stop — I give up," Bob cried, flopping back in his seat. "What did I do to deserve this?"

Carter laughed. "Okay, it's not you, but you own property that you rent out. You have to deal with the public every day so you can't come out looking like the bad guy in this."

Bob didn't seem moved by his logic.

"You know I'm right."

"I know. I know," he finally admitted. "So how do I get out of this hole I dug myself into?"

"That I can show you," Carter told him with a grin. "I have it all right here."

He unrolled the blueprints and set Bob's phone and a paperweight on the upper corners to hold them down. Bob held one lower one and Carter held the other as he stood at Bob's side. "This is a simple solution at not much cost, and it will solve everyone's problems."

"This is your idea for a back entrance to the dog shop to keep the dogs off the walkway."

"No, it's not exactly mine. Terri suggested it, and I think it's a good idea." Carter explained how it would work and the advantages to the shop with a window into the kitchen for the public to watch the baker. "The parking and grassy areas outside won't need to be changed, and they're perfect for dogs and right beside the entrance."

"So how much is this going to cost us?"

"Let's just say that it'll cost a lot less than going to court to defend an eviction notice," Carter said, pulling out the sheets with the construction and landscaping costs. He'd left out any information he had from Terri about her not being able to afford the attorney to fight M&S.

"Is that all? Are you sure?" Bob asked looking up at him.

"That's all because we're just building a new hallway to the existing back door into the shop. Terri said that if she had to, she would sacrifice the space from the kitchen for the hallway. That means all the construction is interior and not that expensive."

"I get it," Bob said after another look. "But you've changed the back door."

"I just beefed it up a little to meet the code and added a sign with the store name too. You want people to use that entrance so it can't just look like a back door that only

employees use like the others down the line.
I think this does it. Since the store is on the
end, it will look like the front door that's
around on the side."

"And this will satisfy her?"

Carter straightened, releasing the blueprints that immediately curled up from the
corner he'd been holding. Bob removed the
weights holding the upper corners and
rolled the sheets up with the cost lists inside.

"That's a hard question for me to answer
at this point," Carter said, walking around
the desk and running his hand through his
hair. "She won't even talk to me, much less
tell me if this is what she had in mind."

"Should I call her?" Bob asked.

"You can't tell her that she can stay if she
agrees to this plan to keep the dogs off the
mall walkway. Besides, I need to repair the
damage this did to us personally, but that'll
only happen when I show her what I've
done to help her to make things right. When
I show her the plans, we'll know if she likes
them."

"But she's not talking to you."

Carter planted his hands on his hips.
"Listen to me. Her pet parade is coming up
fast. I thought I'd enter Fred and try to talk
to her afterwards."

"Wouldn't it be better to ask her to come

here to the offices?"

Carter shook his head. "Right now she doesn't trust me and doesn't want to have anything to do with me. She probably thinks I was a part of the decision to evict her and purposely didn't tell her. So I have to get her to believe in me first. Then we'll stand a better chance of her believing in what I'm trying to do for her to keep K-Nine Treats in Riverside."

"Good luck. I sure don't want this whole eviction thing to blow up and hit the newspapers again like it did in connection to the parade." He shook his head. "I've got to give her credit. She hit us in the one spot where it hurts the most. If she turns public opinion against us any more, the city might think again about the permissions we need to build Riverside Two."

"Don't even think that," Carter insisted as he took the drawings and headed for the door. Standing in the doorway, he turned back. "She really wants to keep her store where it is, and I want to keep her in my life. I'm counting on being able to do both — with the help of my dog." He grinned. Besides having a ton of work to do, he had to figure out a costume for Fred to wear. Suddenly, he reversed his direction and bent over Bob's wastebasket.

"What are you doing?" Bob asked.

The drawings tucked under his arm, Carter pulled the discarded newspaper out and laid it back on Bob's desk. "Do you have scissors?"

Opening his desk, Bob handed him a pair. Carter cut the form in the corner below the article on the parade.

"Thanks. I need this entry form to join in the parade," he said, slipping it in his shirt pocket.

"Ah, Carter?"

"Yeah?"

"You should do something else too, before the parade."

"What's that?"

"Get some sleep. You look like hell. They'll think you're in ghoulish makeup already."

Carter nodded. "Thanks a bunch, my friend. But now that these are done, I guess I could go back to my old schedule that included some time sleeping," he said with a wry smile before resuming his path down the hall to his office.

"Have you decided what to dress the puppies up as?" Terri heard Sue ask.

"It'll just be something simple. I'm putting red print handkerchiefs around their necks and setting them in a red wagon with fence-like sides so they don't fall or jump out."

"Do you mean the one Tom uses to bring in sacks of meal?"

"Right. I bought it to use to carry stuff into the shop when I first opened. It saved my back a lot of strain."

"I don't get it. What do farmers' handkerchiefs have to do with a wagon?"

Terri smiled. "You'll have to read the sign on the wagon:

'Ready, Willing, and Able:
Rescued dogs make great pets.'

That should explain it."

Sue laughed. "That's perfect, and it will be a great ad for adopting rescued dogs."

"And I hope it will be good for the program in general. Maybe we'll get some more volunteers to care for rescued dogs until they find homes for them."

The kitchen door swung open and Tom headed for them. "How's this?" He held out his hands to display a dog-bone treat lying on his palms. About four inches long, it had a neon orange bow tied around it with a tag stapled on the end of one strand of the ribbon.

Terri lifted the tag and read,

212

" 'Treat the dogs in our town's animal shelter to a bone. For every one purchased today at K-Nine Treats, we will donate one to the shelter.' "

"That looks great," Terri told him. "Can you have them ready for the day of the parade?"

"They'll be ready," Tom promised.

"At the rate you're baking them, we could supply the shelter for some time," Sue commented with a grin. "But count on me to help tie the bows. I'll bet our puppy volunteers would help too."

"That sounds great. They can start at any time because they'll keep," Tom replied. "And the way things sell here, I'm always playing catch-up anyway. It would be nice to get ahead."

The bell on the shop door tinkled and he looked up. "Oh, here's your committee. I'll get back to the ovens before I burn any."

"Thanks, Tom," Terri called before turning to welcome the women instrumental in helping her get the Costumed-Pet Parade off and running.

"Break it to me gently," Terri told them with a grin. "How many do we have now?"

"You're not going to believe this," Linda, the registration committee head said. Her face was bright with a broad smile. "We have forty-six entries so far, and it's still a week away."

"Oh, no," Terri groaned. "That's great, but what are we going to do with them all?" She could imagine the chaos they could create with all the animals in one place.

"Not to worry," Sally, who compiled the list of volunteers, told her. "I have eighteen volunteers to line the route and keep things moving along. They'll be here two hours ahead of the start of the parade to put up the fluorescent pink tape along the route to keep the animals on the right path."

She chuckled. "That many volunteers will also make the audience look larger, though I don't think there's a chance that we won't have a viewing crowd on our hands."

"It's wonderful to have so much help," Terri said. "I could never do it without all of you. Thank you."

"It's our pleasure," one of the women replied.

"And it's fun for us. Oh, Harry has another article in this weekend's paper about the parade," Mary, the publicity chairperson said, "only, this time he's saying that the 'First Annual' part might be 'One and Only' because of the eviction notice you received. And he's stating M&S's plan to keep dogs

214

off the walkway. That ought to move more public opinion to your side."

Terri felt a sharp pain in the area of her conscience. "Won't it be awfully harsh seeing that in print?"

"You're not going soft on us now, are you?" Sally asked.

Terri took a deep breath. "No, I want to keep my shop right here," she replied.

"We're helping you fight them because we want you to stay here too," Mary said. "Nobody wants a war with them, and don't worry — Harry won't state anything but the bare facts."

Terri nodded as the phone rang. After hearing his voice, she said, "Hi, Sam. What's up?"

"Hi yourself. I'm just calling to say that we'd like to join in your parade with an official Riverside County Animal Shelter entry and that the local Dogs for the Blind group would like to, as well."

"That's great. The farmer with the Labs I took care of will be there as an example of puppies raised to try out for their program. And of course, I'm putting the puppies I still have in with a sign about rescued dogs, but the more the merrier. What are you bringing?"

"You won't believe them until you see

them. They are matching and gorgeous. A woman just brought them in this morning. She said they got bigger than she expected and she can't handle them anymore."

"What breed are they?"

"I think they're pure standard poodle. She thought she was buying toy poodles. She said she couldn't tell the difference as puppies."

"Oh, dear — that's a big mistake," Terri put in with a laugh.

"Yeah, but people buying puppies from anyone other than accredited breeders don't always get told the truth. Anyway, these are beautiful. Betty over at the Clip Joint gave them show-poodle cuts, and they're ready. She even had a tiara and a tutu for each one that her grandchildren used to play with. So we're in costume and good to go."

"That's wonderful. They'll give the parade a lot of class," Terri told him with a laugh. "I think you'll be a hit."

"We'll be there a half hour before it starts, okay?" Sam asked.

"That's perfect. You can help if there's a problem with a dog."

"I'd be happy to. I'll wear my uniform and protective gear. That ought to get a laugh walking with these two dainty ladies in pink tutus."

216

Laughing, Terri said good-bye and hung up the phone. After explaining to the committee heads about the poodles and the Labs joining in, she volunteered herself and the puppies to bring up the rear instead of heading it. She told the committee that her neighbor Marty had agreed to walk with her and take over the puppies in case Terri got called to help with something else.

"Now let's put our heads together and arrange the other entries according to the breed of animals they're bringing. We can add the entries as they come in. I have nightmares of dogs chasing cats that slide free from their harnesses and race up trees so that the fire department has to come in with a ladder to get them down."

"That's a little bit more excitement than we want," Sue said with a grin.

"Yeah, it's a lot more than I want," Terri agreed.

They split up the entry forms and started sorting them according to whether it was dog, or cat, or whatever, and then for the next hour they discussed the order.

"The judges will love this. I'm sure glad I'm not one," Sue put in.

"Have we heard from all the judges?" Terri asked as they finished.

"I'm sure the mayor would do it," Mary said.

"And the president of the Community Bank would," Linda added. "He's always looking for a chance to appear in public."

"Oh, and that disc jockey for the early morning show at the radio station has already agreed to be a judge. I listen to him every day while I'm getting the kids' breakfasts," Sue recommended. "He seemed to be very excited to be asked."

Terri wrote the names down. "Three judges should be a good number, but in case one can't make it, how about another back-up suggestion?"

"Hmm, how about the lease agent at M&S?" Sue put in with a laugh. The other women groaned.

"Let's see. We've got a representative from government, finance, and entertainment. Too bad Sam is going to be in the parade with his poodles. He would make a great judge."

"But I'll bet he gets more news coverage for the shelter by being in the parade," Mary said with a grin.

"All right, then, who else could we ask?"

The ladies listed some more names that included the pastor of the huge downtown church that was walking distance from

Riverside and the Chief of Police.

"I'm betting one of them will do it," Terri said.

"And as soon as you have the commitment, call me and Harry will put them in the article for this weekend."

"That would be wonderful. Wow, this is really coming together. I can't thank you enough for all your help," Terri told the women, who rose from their seats to leave. "Oh, and Linda, be sure and keep me apprised of the number registered."

"I'll do that," she agreed before leaving. "I already got the ones from Sue that were left here at the store."

"This is going to be fun," Sue said as they put the chairs and benches back in place by the dogs' feeding area.

"I just hope this works and I can stay here," Terri said.

CHAPTER TEN

After reading the business rental classifieds for weeks and doing nothing about seeing any of them, Terri knew the time had come. She had to quit stalling, counting on a miracle, and get out and look at some other properties.

Her first step was to drive to several listed and look them over on her own. For the most part, the adventure turned out to be depressing. The vacancies were mostly in small strip malls where there were few cars parked that might indicate customers in the shops.

One looked fairly interesting, but the space was so large that she thought she could open a bowling alley in addition to her shop. She would have to invest too much in stock to ever fill it, and then she would need extra staff to cover it.

But unable to give up, she returned to her shop. After a few minutes of quality time with the dogs and puppies, she called a realtor who specialized in business properties. Explaining the eviction notice, she said she needed to find another suitable shop location. Once she understood what Terri wanted, they discussed some of the possibilities.

"I could take you to see these this afternoon," the realtor, whose name was Janet, offered. "I had the time blocked out for a couple coming from out of town, but they called yesterday to cancel."

"That would be good. Where can I meet you?"

"I'll pick you up in twenty minutes. You can look through the book as we drive between the available properties."

"That sounds fine. I'll come out to the parking lot and stand near the walkway entrance. You can pick me up there," Terri replied, adding a brief description of the pinstripe brown slacks and pale beige sweater she wore under her trench coat.

As she hung up the phone, she felt as if a vise were tightening around her chest. She looked out the one-way mirror beside her desk and scanned the shop. She loved it all, and she loved everything that she did here. She remembered the week before she opened that she spent putting up the shelves and bins. Thanks to her father, who had taught her how to use a hammer and saw, she had saved a lot of money by creating the display space she needed without using expensive ready-made units. The metal bins she'd found at a farm supply store gave the store a distinctive look that said clean, healthy pets. Now with the shelves full, and dog and cat garments artistically displayed above them, she thought it looked every bit as good as it could have looked with a purchased display.

Glancing at her watch, Terri had to cut her daydreaming short. Passing through the shop, she accepted Sue's wish for good luck and went out to meet Janet.

Already waiting for her, Janet introduced herself and opened the car door for her. She handed Terri a thick loose-leaf binder the moment she was settled in the passenger seat with her seatbelt fastened. "These are business rentals and sales that are available in the county," Janet told her as she opened the book about at the mid-point. "The rentals start at this tab. You can look through them while I drive to the first one I'd like to show you." She pulled out of the parking lot and headed north.

Terri turned the pages looking only at the location, square footage and rental rate for

222

each one. "These are less expensive than the rent I'm paying now," she commented.

"You're in a prime location and the rents match. Even at their rates, I know M&S has a waiting list for spaces."

"Yes, so they say," Terri murmured, remembering that Bob had told her he had someone waiting who could be in her space and up and running by Christmas. She sighed and went back to the book.

"I drove by a few of these this morning. The strip malls seemed to be void of customers."

"They're all feeling the pinch since Riverside was finished. And when they finish the new section, it won't get any better, I'm afraid," Janet said, shaking her head. "But your shop is so unique that it would attract customers wherever it is," she added more brightly.

"But I wonder if it would ever draw as many as I have now," Terri wondered. "Isn't the rule of real estate 'location, location, location'?"

"Yeah," Janet said more softly. "But you can't stay in that location, can you?"

Terri sighed and looked out the side window. No, she probably couldn't stay where she was. She had built her store from nothing twice before, and she could do it again. The third time was the charm, wasn't it?

She already had a loyal group of customers. If she moved closer to residential areas, she might attract even more families with pets who hadn't gone downtown to Riverside to find her.

As Janet pulled up to the first storefront they were going to inspect, Terri felt better about her prospects. Determined to turn a raw deal into something positive, she climbed out of the car and followed Janet inside.

Janet turned out to be very accommodating. She waited patiently while Terri talked to store clerks and owners next to each of the places they viewed. None of them gave a very positive outlook on the empty spaces she'd seen, but they were all very enthusiastic about the possibility of having her as a new tenant in their mall. Terri was a bit surprised at how many of them already knew about her shop, but realized it was thanks to the recent newspaper coverage of the parade. During each visit, she took notes and copied the vital statistics about each storefront from Janet's book.

"Sorry I can't loan you the book, but I can't let that out of my sight."

"That's okay," Terri assured her. "I can

understand exactly what it's like to have something your whole business depends on taken from you. And I've got all the info I need."

Later, back at the shop, Terri asked Sue's advice about the reputation of each of the areas where she'd viewed a potential property. Sue, who had a family to shop for, knew a lot more about each shopping area than Terri. Tom came out from the kitchen to put in his two cents' worth, and between the three of them, they narrowed it down to the two best places that Terri wanted to go look at again.

Before she did that, however, she wanted to spend a little more time driving around town to see if some other possibility popped out at her. She had toyed with the possibility of renting a place that included living quarters. That would save her the rent she paid on an apartment, she thought. Before she moved into Riverside, she had thought about having a small kennel business where people could bring their pets when they went out of town for short stays in addition to the shop and dog bakery. She'd even thought of renting out an area in the shop to someone who did pet grooming. But she'd never gone ahead to figure out what that would involve.

More space would give her more room for the puppies she cared for. Living in the same building as the business meant the puppies wouldn't have to intrude on her personal space, and yet they would be close enough to keep a careful eye on them. Maybe there was a house on a street that had been zoned for commercial use. Or perhaps there was a place on the outskirts of town where it would be quieter to live than on a busy city street and there would be more parking space available.

Thinking along these lines gave her a lot more details to consider. She'd have to start with contacting the city zoning and health officials about the laws concerning keeping animals that paid their way, and about the grooming too.

Smiling, Terri realized that with all these possibilities opening again for her, the vise that had been clamping her chest no longer troubled her. She had to develop a good business plan that didn't call for being located at Riverside. But with so few weeks left in which to do it, she first had to figure out how to pack five or six more hours into each day.

On Tuesday, the day before the deadline for registering an entry into the parade, K-Nine

Treats' door opened and the little bells jingled. Sue looked up to see a tall, handsome man with dark hair enter. He wore gray trousers and a blazer over a pinstriped shirt that was open at the neck. He looked around carefully in a way she imagined a thief would when he was casing the shop in order to burglarize it later. But she quickly decided he wasn't the type. A man dressed like that did not go around robbing pet-supply shops.

Night and Day had grown restless in their run and stood with their paws in the links. When Day barked a couple of times, she shushed him. He quieted but didn't lose interest in the new customer.

"Can I help you?" she asked the man with her usual smile.

"Oh, yes, thank you."

Walking over to the counter behind which she stood, he pulled a scrap of crinkled newsprint from his pocket. She recognized it at once as the entry form for the parade. She guessed that he was probably going to register his kids with their family dog. He unfolded the form and handed it to her.

"Thanks," she said. Though she didn't read each line, she scanned it to be sure he had filled in all the blanks with information where they needed it. "I see you have a black Lab. Well, it looks like what I need is all here." She handed him a sheet with the starting time and location. "Be sure he's on a properly fitted leash. There will be a lot of animals gathering by the river, and we don't want any to be on the loose."

He laughed. "No, I'll bet you don't. That would be chaos."

She scanned the form again to the top where she read his name for the first time. "Well, thank you, ah . . . Mr. Morris." The name sank in and she jerked her head up to meet his gaze. "You're Carter Morris?"

"Yes, I am. Is there a problem with that?"

"Well, no . . . I . . . ah . . . no," she stuttered. "You want to be in the parade?"

"My dog Fred does."

Quickly glancing at the one-way glass window to Terri's office, she looked back to meet his gaze. He glanced in that direction too and raised his eyebrows in question. She shook her head.

"No, she's not in. She had to take the puppies for one last visit to the vet. They'll all be going up for adoption next week." She shrugged. "Everything happens at once, but at least she won't have to move them when your company kicks us out," she added with venom that she didn't try to hide.

"I'm doing my best to prevent that from happening, and you could help me." He lifted a roll of paper she hadn't noticed was in his other hand. "Would you give me a minute to voice your opinion of these drawings?"

"What do you mean? What are they?"

"They're drawings of this shop with the new rear entrance that Terri told me would keep her customers' dogs off the walkway in front of the other stores."

"She told me about her idea but said M&S didn't buy it. Why would you design it when you're kicking her out?"

"I have nothing to do with kicking her out. That's all my partner's department." Shaking his head, he spread out the drawings. "I just thought it would be worth some of my personal time to do the drawings in case the new entrance would solve the problems so she could stay here."

Gazing at his face as he turned the drawings toward her, she didn't see any guile, but she knew Terri had good reason for being so angry and disappointed with him.

"Here's the present wall of the kitchen, and here's the new hallway to a rear entrance. With a little shift, a new door and sign, it will look better as an entrance, and not like a back door."

Sue studied the plans and pictured the new area. "That grassy area is handy for walking the dogs instead of going down to the grassy slope toward the river."

"I noticed you have a dispenser roll of plastic bags out front to take to clean up after the dogs. That's a great public service."

"We could always put another stand holder at the back door," Sue told him as she went back to studying the drawings.

"I put in the window Terri wanted here in the hall so the customers could view the kitchen. I could even add a platform across there for kids to stand on. How does that strike you?"

Chuckling, she said, "Tom, our baker, would like that. He gets lonesome back there 'cause we're always so busy. He'd like the company."

As if on cue, two customers came in. One was carrying a small lapdog that was all long hair and very little dog. They headed directly for the grooming products and the display of brushes and bows.

"I have to go help those ladies. Is there anything else you wanted to know?" Sue asked Carter.

"No, now we just have to get a meeting of the minds on the project. For that I have to get Terri to talk to me." He shook his head.

"But thank you." He rolled up the sheets. "Fred and I will see you Saturday at the parade."

Sue smiled as he left, but she had to wonder what Terri would say when she discovered that Carter was bringing his dog to the parade. Should she warn her that he was coming? Or should she not mention his visit at all? Did Terri even know he was working on drawings for a new entrance?

As she strode over to the ladies to see if they needed help picking out a comb or brush, she thought how thankful she was that she was married. It was a lot easier than being single.

Carter had worked on the specifications for the addition to Riverside so late that when the phone rang in the middle of the night, he had barely gotten asleep. "This had better be important," he growled into the receiver.

"Carter, is that you?"

"Yeah — who's this?" He swung his feet down to the floor and sat up on the edge of the bed.

"It's me, Sam — the Animal Rescue officer that Terri introduced you to when you came out to help her with the Lab puppies."

"Oh, sure, now I remember you. What's

up at this hour?"

"Yeah, I'm sorry about the hour, but I need help and I can't seem to reach Terri. Her phone is constantly busy."

"Maybe she took it off the hook," Carter suggested. "She probably wanted a little insurance for a night's sleep."

"That's too bad. She has the best luck with the little ones, and I got a big batch of them this time. I need all the help I can get. We raided a puppy farm, and the ones that are still alive are more than we can handle at the shelter."

"What can I do to help?"

"Well, since I can't get ahold of Terri, you could come get the pups and take them to her, I suppose." He chuckled. "But unless you've got papers or blankets in your car, it will never be the same again."

"Let me try to get Terri," Carter said with a chuckle. "Maybe she doesn't know and just has a phone off the hook. Do you have a cell phone number?"

"Sure, and I'll give you the address too. If you find her, just come straight out here."

Carter took the number and address down and ended the call. It took only minutes for him to dress. He grabbed his keys and pulled on his old jacket. Before he left, he tried her number just in case. He got a busy signal.

"Hang up the phone, Terri," he muttered as he grabbed a stack of newspapers from the recycle bin in the kitchen cabinet. Looking around the room, he saw nothing else that would help. Well, if he couldn't find Terri, he'd think of something.

Fred sat by the door expecting to go too. Carter petted his head and ordered him to stay. "You go back to sleep. At least one of us will get some sleep, my friend."

With that, he was out the door and on his way to Terri's apartment. He jogged up the stairs instead of waiting for the elevator and rang her bell. Barking excitedly, Night and Day raced to the door. Knowing the dogs were okay, Carter breathed a little easier as thoughts of a leaky gas pipe on the stove flew out of his mind along with the vision of Terri out cold on the floor with the phone in her hand trying to call for help.

He leaned on the buzzer again and then heard a sleepy Terri call out that she was coming. Clutching the lapels of a thick terry robe together across her chest, she opened the door to the width allowed by the safety chain and peered out at him.

"Carter, it's the middle of the night. What on earth are you doing here?"

"Sam called me. He's been trying to call you. Your phone must be off the hook because he just gets a busy signal. I told him I'd come help him, but I wanted to try to find you first."

"I haven't been on the phone." She frowned for a moment and then looked down at Night and Day. "Not again," she said shaking her head. "Just a minute."

Closing the door, she unhooked the chain and then opened it. "Come on in. It'll just take a few minutes for me to get dressed."

Carter strode into the living room while Terri went to dress.

"Say, check the phone in there," she called from the bedroom. "That's the one the dogs knock off the cradle once in a while. It's on the end table — at least that's where it should be."

Carter saw the end of the receiver peeking out from under the skirt of the couch. He picked it up and replaced it on the base. Lifting it again moments later, he heard a dial tone.

"That's the one," he called to Terri. "It was on the floor."

"I've got to remember to put it up on the bookcase instead of on the end table," she called from the bedroom. "I was using it earlier this evening and left it where they could reach it. I guess the boys like toys they can knock on the floor and hear a buzzing sound."

Dressed in her old jeans and sweatshirt with a stack of towels in her arms, she marched past him to the foyer closet where she pulled on her jacket.

"It's cold tonight. You might want hat and gloves," Carter suggested.

Nodding, she reached up to the closet shelf for her knit beret and gloves. Those on, she grabbed a handful of disposable rubber gloves and turned to hand him two. "Okay, I'm all set."

"You know, I don't know another woman who could have gotten ready so fast," Carter told her with a grin. "I just wish you had been that eager to be with me rather than to go rescue puppies."

She met his gaze for a few moments and then turned to open the door. "We'd better hurry," she said as if he had said nothing that required any comment from her.

Stepping through the door, she turned back to him. He picked up the towels she had left on the hall table and stepped through the door to wait while she locked it.

"Thanks," she muttered.

They hurried down the stairs in silence.

Outside, they agreed to ride in her car though she accepted his offer of the stack of newspapers he had brought.

"You can never have too many," she told him. "Despite all my neighbors giving me theirs, I still run out sometimes."

Fifteen minutes later, they arrived at the address brightly lit by the flashing lights on the police and rescue vehicles.

CHAPTER ELEVEN

"You found her," Sam said, shaking hands with Carter.

"My phone was off the hook. Sorry about that," Terri put in.

"Well, I'm glad you're here. You couldn't have taken them much sooner anyway. There were so many injured and sick that I called the vet. She's doing some triage to see which ones go to the volunteers and which ones go back to the animal hospital with her. She's out back."

Sam led the way behind the two-story house that sat on wooded land about a city block from its nearest neighbor. Behind the house, a separate building, originally a two-car garage, sat at the end of the driveway. The wide car door had been raised.

Huge floodlights illuminated the horrid conditions under which the owner had been raising puppies. The garage walls were lined with layers of metal cages, each one stacked

237

right over another. The cement floor ran with pet waste.

In the center area, the vet bent over a litter of puppies that an officer had just removed one at a time from one of the pens. He wore thick leather gloves to keep from getting bitten, but the puppies' mother, who still lay in the pen, had not even raised her head to object to his taking her babies.

"I think you'd better look at that one. She's non-responsive," he told the vet.

"Not another one," the vet said as she rose wearily and walked to the pen. She felt for a heartbeat and then listened to the chest. "I need water. Bring me that cage feeder, Terri, will you?"

While Carter didn't know what a cage feeder was, Terri picked up a bottle of water that had a metal spout coming out the bottom. Carter could see it was the kind that a small animal would lick on the tip to make water drip out onto its tongue.

"She's alive, but so dehydrated she can hardly move. Hold it up to her mouth for now. I'll give her intravenous fluids when we get her to the hospital."

"What about her pups?" Terri asked.

"They're good to go, I think," the vet replied. "She's given them her all, that's for sure. They're in better shape than most, but

238

they should be fed right away."

"Why don't you take those, Terri?" Sam asked. "I see another volunteer coming now, and the van should be back to make a second run to the shelter any minute now."

"Okay, I'll do that," Terri told him.

Carter moved to help as Terri swung into action. "I'll get the basket," she said. Running to her car, she retrieved the basket and returned. Tossing Carter one of the towels, she said, "Dry them off and try to get as much of the filth off them here as you can. But be careful of their paws. They'll be tender."

"Why will they be tender?"

"It's because of their having nothing but that chicken wire fencing for a floor on the cage. Sometimes it's sharp enough to cut their soft pads, and it makes them sore just standing on it all the time."

They worked in silence until the six puppies were cleaned and set on a clean towel in the basket. Carter picked up the basket and set it in the back of Terri's car as a man got out of the car that had just pulled into the driveway.

Hanging back by Terri's car, Carter watched as she warmly greeted the man. Shaking hands, he didn't release hers as they laughed and talked for a few moments.

Carter shifted his weight onto his other foot and frowned. Whoever this guy was, Carter didn't like him hanging on to Terri's hand like that.

But suddenly, Terri and the newcomer were all business. Sam joined them and walked with the man toward the garage. Terri called out her good-byes and jogged toward her car.

"Who's he?" Carter asked. He'd sounded gruff, which he hadn't meant it to sound, but Terri didn't seem to notice.

"That's Vicki's husband. He doesn't like her to be out alone on these jobs in the middle of the night. He stays home until his niece can come over to sleep on the couch to be there in case their kids need something. Then he always comes to join her."

"Who's Vicki?" Carter asked.

"She's the vet."

"Oh." Carter climbed into the passenger seat as Terri sat behind the wheel. He fastened his seatbelt and looked over at her when she didn't start the car right away.

"Thanks, Carter, for helping me again tonight despite all that's going on with us. I . . . I really appreciate it."

Grinning, he replied, "I'm glad I could do it. I like helping you, and I'm glad you can still think of you and me as *us*. We make a good team."

She looked at him a few moments longer, and he thought he saw tears welling in her eyes, highlighted by the flashing red and white lights on the squad cars. But she blinked rapidly and without saying more, she looked out the windshield and started the car.

Six puppies to clean up and feed were a lot harder than two times the three little ones that Terri was already taking care of.

"Having to make up the formula takes time, but we've got to finish feeding these guys before I . . ." she said. A huge yawn stopped her and she laughed. "I'm glad these are the last ones."

Carter rose and set his fed puppy with his siblings in the paper-lined plastic pen where the Labs had been kept. The solid floor softened with newspaper and old towels would feel a lot better on their little paws than the bare chicken wire fencing had, he thought. He stepped aside a little as Terri set hers in with the rest who were all sleeping.

"They are so cute. How could anyone treat them so badly?" she said in little more than a whisper.

"They should be thankful that there are good people like you who help them with

241

no thought at losing sleep."

She raised a hand to cover another yawn. "We're both losing sleep tonight. You go home. There's no reason for you to lose more. I'm just going to rinse these bottles and wash them."

"You're sure you don't need more help?" he asked.

"Thanks, but no."

Following her to the door, he shrugged on his jacket and stood with his hand on the knob. Their gazes met and he wanted to kiss her good night. "Well, good night, Terri."

"Good night. And . . . and thanks."

Not giving her time to object, he lifted her chin with a bent finger and kissed her. Encouraged by the feeling of her lips softening and responding to his, he wanted to continue the kiss, but knew he shouldn't. Instead, he lifted his head and held her gaze for a few more moments. Then, releasing her chin, he turned and left the apartment.

Terri closed and locked the door after Carter left and then leaned against it. She listened until his footfalls disappeared down the apartment hallway and then she trudged into the kitchen where she washed the bottles and filled them for the morning.

Finally done, she removed her clothes and pulled the warm knit nightgown over her

242

head that she had been sleeping in before Carter had woken her.

Climbing into bed, she had to wonder how such a nice man who she had come to care dearly for, who had been such a treat to meet and be with, who was a wonderful kisser, had pulled such a mean trick on her.

"Will you look at all those people?" Terri said as she stood by the area of the parking lot that had been roped off to make room for all the entrants.

"All but three of the fifty-eight people who registered have shown up," Linda, the volunteer who helped so much with the registration said.

"It's just about time to start. Are the judges in place?"

"They're close. The mayor is still busy shaking hands, but Mary's over there. She'll make sure they are seated and ready when the parade begins."

Terri wiped her palms on her thighs. She was happy she'd decided against dressing up and worn comfortable jeans instead. She'd already kneeled on the ground to help entrants. A pantsuit would have been ruined by now.

"Ms. Bookman, Ms. Bookman," she heard a man calling from behind her.

She turned to see Pierre from the restaurant in the middle of Riverside waving to catch her attention. In his chef's uniform consisting of brightly patterned black-and-white pants with a white coat and tall hat, he ran to her side. "I must come and tell you," he said in his French accent. "I have the full restaurant for lunch and again a seating in the afternoon. The parade is so good to bring the people."

Terri grinned. "I'm glad your business is good," she said kindly.

"Oh, yes, I have added the tall heaters and we have the tables outside on the walkway now. It takes long time to get the permission, but now we do it until is too cold."

"Is it warm enough even now?"

"With the heaters it is. Next spring and summer it will be very special to eat there on the walkway in the warm air."

"It sounds like it will be lovely overlooking the river."

"And you must do the parade again next year to keep the peoples coming in," he replied.

Taking a deep breath, she shook her head. "I don't know if I can. In case you haven't heard, I got an eviction notice. They said the other shop owners didn't like having dogs around all the time. If the owners of

Riverside have their way, I won't be here next year."

"Oh, but you must," he insisted. "I not like the dogs at first, but now they bring in the peoples. I will tell them it is big mistake to make you leave."

"Thank you, Pierre. I hope you do because I like it here. I'd like to stay."

Sue ran over to her side and stopped their conversation. "The parade is ready to begin. The judges are ready at their table, and there are photographers from three newspapers here," she said excitedly.

"Thanks," Terri said to her. "Excuse me, but I've got to go," she said to Pierre.

She and Sue jogged to the head of the line where Marty stood by the wagon that contained her three rescued puppies. All three pups had made it through the difficult weeks, and all were ready to be adopted. Her newly acquired rescued dogs were more fragile, and she'd left them in the shop under the watchful eye of the part-time clerks. Her own two dogs waited less than patiently and jumped up on her when she reached them.

"Down," she said sharply. The dogs obeyed, but she knew she really had to spend more time training them. She wasn't setting a very good example.

"Here you go," she said, handing her the wagon handle. "Everyone wants you to lead the parade, Terri, not end it. This is for your benefit and you've worked so hard on it."

"We'll come right behind you," Sam said, the dainty ballerina poodles on each side.

"And I'll stay here to keep people in an orderly line," Tom offered. "You go and don't worry about the others following. They will."

Terri grinned. "You think so, huh? Well, let's get this show on the road."

Leading the parade with the puppies wearing their farmer's handkerchiefs tied around their necks and the sign on the wagon, she slowly walked across the parking lot to the path that sloped down to the river. Marty walked behind the wagon ready to pull it if Terri needed to leave.

Night and Day pranced happily at Terri's side. Day wore a tee shirt with the K-Nine Treats logo and had dark glasses perched on her head, while Night had on a ruffled pajama top and two curlers in her topknot. The woman who sewed coats to sell in the shop had made the costumes for her. The curlers never left her head, and Terri wondered if Sue had used glue when she'd dressed them. Nah, that wasn't possible, she concluded.

At the river she turned and walked along the river on a path parallel to the cement walkway in front of the stores at the top of the slope. The slope and the edge of the walkway at the top were nearly filled with spectators and supporters who waved and cheered for the entrant of their choice.

As she rounded the curve to follow the river, she looked back at the long line of costumed pets and their owners. She was surprised to see that a dozen of her loyal customers were dispersed in the line. Each carried a sign supporting her shop and objecting to the eviction. At several points she saw them stop and talk to the bystanders who had pointed at the signs and called out questions about them. She hadn't realized they were going to do that. It had never been her intention to embarrass M&S. She just wanted them to cancel the eviction notice.

Among the bystanders she saw the elderly women from the housing project that didn't allow pets. They waved and smiled and applauded when they saw Terri had noticed them. Just beyond the judges' stand where they would be assured of being in any photos that were taken, there were several teenagers holding up a long strip of fabric that read, "Keep K-9 Treats at Riverside."

She could easily forgive them for abbreviating her shop's name.

Tears burned in the backs of her eyes, as she felt nearly overwhelmed by the huge public support. If only the display would change the minds of the powers that be at M&S. Then she would have everything she ever wanted.

Well, that wasn't exactly true.

She wanted to be with Carter, but she didn't see how that could happen now. Blinking away the burning sensation, she waved at the judges as she passed. They were busy watching for the entrants with their numbers displayed on their backs. Each held a clipboard with the numbers on sheets with room for their comments. She didn't envy their job. It wasn't going to be easy.

How anyone could pick from a full-sized black poodle-witch with spiked hair plus pointed hat and cape, a retired greyhound racer in his racing colors, an unhappy cat in a leopard suit, and a long dachshund that sported a foam hotdog bun on his sides and a ribbon of fake mustard zigzagging along his back, Terri couldn't imagine.

At the end of the path, Terri handed the wagon handle to Marty. "Take it the rest of the way around, okay?"

"Okay, I'll do that."

Terri walked up the hill to the walkway. She wanted to go back and see the rest of the parade and she knew the other entrants did too. As the parade reached the end of the path, the participants all filled in the open spaces on the slope. Terri headed to middle, uphill but not far from the judges' table.

The volunteers, who raised dogs in the first months of their lives for the Dogs for the Blind program, were a hit and earned a round of applause. About in the middle of the lineup was the K-9 unit from the state police department.

And just beyond them was a man leading a black Lab in a superman costume that bore a sign noting he was a retired Seeing Eye dog. The man sported an artful cardboard doghouse on his shoulders, created so his head was visible in the open doorway.

It was Carter — in the doghouse.

Terri had to laugh right along with the rest of the spectators. But then he veered off the parade path and came right toward her. Of their own volition, her feet began to move backwards, away from him. The boys, with her while Marty took the wagon, jumped and barked in anticipation of seeing Fred again. Terri's hands felt clammy as her heart raced. He quickly caught up to her and she stopped.

"Hi," he said with a smile on his face.

"Hi, yourself. That's a nice costume."

A glance around told her that the two of them had suddenly gotten more interesting to watch than the parade. Before she looked back at him he must have realized the same thing because she felt him take her hand in one of his as he maneuvered them up to the walkway, away from the crowd, where they stopped.

"Stay," he told Fred in a firm voice.

He dropped Fred's leash, and the dog didn't move despite her dogs playing around him, enticing him to join in the fun. Untying two straps under his armpits, Carter lifted the doghouse off over his head. He set it on the ground and Terri's dogs moved from jumping on Fred to exploring the colorfully painted house.

"Come on out of there," she said, pulling on their leashes.

"It's okay. It's going right into the recycle bin now that you've let me out."

"I've let you out?"

"You've released me from the doghouse."

"Carter, I don't think . . ."

"I know. I know. I was just teasing, and maybe it was not appropriate because I consider what is happening to us to be very serious and not a joke. It's too important to me. Terri, you're important to me."

She had to look away. That stubborn strand of hair had fallen over his forehead and it was all she could do to keep from finger-combing it back again. Chiding herself silently, she had to wonder how she could still be attracted to a man whose company was set on doing her so much harm and causing her so much grief. But she was.

"What is it you want?" she asked without looking up at him.

"This is what I want." He spread out his hands palms up. "I want to talk to you."

"Okay, you've talked to me. Now I have to get back to the parade."

"It's quite a success."

"Yes, it is."

"Look at the walkway. People are going in and out of the shops as well as watching the parade. The shop owners have got to be happy about that."

"Yes, I hope so. Now, if you'll excuse me . . ."

"No, I mean I need to talk to you some more."

"Carter, I don't think we have anything left to say."

"I do, and I have something to show you."

"Show me?"

"Yes, so will you go out to dinner with me tonight? You pick the place. I don't care where it is as long as it's somewhere we can talk, and I can show you what I have."

The parade had ended and all the entrants had added to the spectators surrounding the judging table. Terri saw Sue running toward them.

"They need you to announce the winners, Terri. Go on. I'll bring the dogs." Sue took the leashes and made her way back to the judges' table. The area of the path opposite it where the parade had passed had been cleared for the announcement of the winners.

Terri looked at Carter then and met his gaze. "I have to go."

"Tonight?" he asked, holding her upper arm so she couldn't move away.

"Carter . . ."

"Please?"

"Okay, I'll see you tonight." She tried to turn away, but still he held her arm with his gentle grip.

"Where will we meet?"

"I don't know. I don't care. I have to go."

"Then I'll pick you up at seven."

"Okay, fine — I'll see you then."

He released her arm then, and the last thing she saw was the smile on his face.

"See you at seven," she heard him call after her as she ran down the slope.

CHAPTER TWELVE

The walk up the slope to her shop after the winning pets had been presented their prizes took Terri nearly a half an hour. So many people wanted to talk to her and congratulate her on a great parade. Many also said they were going to call M&S and urge them to let her keep her shop where it was. One junior high teacher wanted her to think about letting her class come and see Tom in action in the kitchen. She hoped Terri could talk about pet nutrition too. Terri urged her to call her at the shop to set it up, and tried to walk on.

"I wanted my children to meet the lady who does so much to help rescued dogs," a mother with two grade-school-aged children in tow said. "We just got Pepper from the dog shelter last month. We would have gotten one at a pet shop if I hadn't come in to your shop to get what we needed and learned about the rescue program. He's just a doll and working out great."

"I'm training him to heel," the older child said. "I work with him every afternoon after school."

"That's wonderful," Terri said, looking at the small dog of questionable ancestry. "Animals from the shelter make wonderful pets, and yours is so cute."

"We tried to dress him up as a fireman, but he wouldn't wear the hat," the boy explained.

"But it fit me, so I wore it," the younger child said.

"Well, it looks cute on you too," Terri said with a grin.

The child, who couldn't quite believe that she had actually spoken to a stranger, hid behind her mother again as Terri moved on.

"Thanks for joining in our parade," Terri said to a family who paused to thank her for organizing it.

"We just had to. We wanted to show our support for your shop. I sure hope M&S lets you stay there."

"Mom wrote a letter to the newspaper," the woman's son said. "Your shop is the best."

"That's wonderful praise and I thank you both. Only time will tell if we can," Terri explained.

"Congratulations!"

Terri felt a hand on her shoulder and turned to see Sally walking beside her. "Sally, how can I ever thank you and all the volunteers you lined up to help? You all did a super job."

"I think it went great, but I think the greyhound dressed like a short clown on stilts should have won," Sally said with a laugh.

"I'm just glad I wasn't a judge. I wouldn't have wanted to be responsible for picking the winners. They were all winners," Terri put in. "Thanks for all your work lining them up and keeping the parade moving."

"I haven't had this much fun in years," Sally replied. "And if you need more help, just let me know. I'm calling into that early morning radio show tomorrow and letting them know how great I think this was and how much our community needs your shop right here where we can get to it easily."

"Thanks, Sally," Terri said, feeling a lump grow in her throat. "Your support means a lot even if, in the end, it doesn't get the eviction cancelled." She swallowed hard and smiled as Sally waved at her friends and veered off in their direction.

Tom came up behind them, his basket, which had been filled with individually wrapped K-Nine Treats, now empty.

"Your treats were sure a hit," Terri told him. "Thanks for all your extra work."

"Well, it sure was more fun than sitting home watching TV on my day off," he said. "And I think everyone had fun."

"No one got bit and I'm very glad of that," Terri said with a laugh.

Her baker laughed and walked on faster when yet more people stopped her to say how great the day had been. Several even took her picture with their children and their costumed pets.

"You have to do this again next year. My kids already have a lot of great ideas for costumes."

"I don't know if I can," Terri said to preface her brief explanation of the eviction notice she had gotten. Before she was done, she had earned more converts to her side in the battle to keep her shop open at Riverside.

By the time she reached the shop, Sue and Tom were both helping the part-time clerks wait on customers. Sue was running the register while the temporary cashier bagged goods and the second part-time clerk helped people find what they were looking for. Tom was replacing stock with whatever he had left in the kitchen.

Mary, whose husband had gone to the newspaper office to write his story while the photographers got the pictures developed, had given the puppies the food that Tom had provided. While they ate, she had collected names and other information from families who had expressed an interest in adopting one of the little guys.

"You'll have to contact the animal shelter," Terri heard her explain. "But I'll give them this list so they'll know you were here and asked about adopting one."

What Terri wanted to do most was sit down for a bit, but after some loving pats for Night and Day, who had come back to the shop with Sue, she took Mary's place by the newly rescued puppies. Now that they were awake, they wanted their bottles. Two hours later, when the store closed, she was more than ready to go home and soak in a hot bath.

"I'm going to sit with my feet up tonight," Sue said as she pulled on her coat to leave. "I feel a take-out pizza coming on for dinner."

That's when Terri remembered that she had promised to go to dinner with Carter. She glanced at her watch. She had less than an hour to get ready.

■ ■ ■ ■

"Bob, we've got to beat them to it," Carter insisted. He'd called Bob and asked him to meet at the office that afternoon.

"This is Saturday — my day off."

But Bob had come reluctantly and in a bad mood that got worse as he listened to all that Carter told him about the parade and public opinion lining up against M&S.

"But if we change our minds about one, they'll all think we won't stick to it if we give out another eviction notice."

Carter shook his head. "Nah, everyone knows this is a special case. The paper even said she's paid all her rent on time and has done nothing to harm the site. They made it clear we're not about to let everyone off the hook."

He ran his hand through his hair to lift the strand off his forehead, but it promptly fell right back down. "Bob, she even had a plastic-bag dispenser at the start of the parade to hand out free bags for people with dogs so they could clean up after them."

Carter watched his partner slump back in his chair.

"All right — she's good people! Oh, I know you're right about canceling the eviction." He shook his head. "I don't see any other way out of this, but I sure would like to save face so we don't come out as the bad guys."

"We can make this a win-win situation if we call the paper now — *right now.* I saw the reporter leave the parade to go back to write his story. There's no local paper tomorrow on Sunday, but it will be in Monday's for sure."

"Okay, I give up. Go ahead and call them," Bob said as he rose and headed for the door.

"The new entrance will be our sincere effort to solve the problem so she can stay — because we really want her there. Are we agreed?"

"You really know how to hit a guy when he's down," Bob groused, "but okay. Say whatever you have to in order to get the public to think we've been trying to help her."

"I have been trying to help her — only she doesn't believe it." Carter rubbed the stiff muscles in the back of his neck.

"I know. So build the hallway. Then if it turns into a pizza joint someday, kids can stand at the window in the hall and watch them make the pizzas. With the rear parking already right there, it will make pick-up service easier."

Carter laughed and shook his head. "I have a feeling that K-Nine Treats will be there a good long time."

"I'm going home to finish mowing my lawn. The fun never ends," he grumbled.

With a wave over his shoulder, Bob left his office and Carter reached for the phone.

The boys announced Carter's arrival at Terri's apartment before she even heard him in the hall. Having barely finished a quick shower once she'd gotten home, she'd pulled on her sweater to match her slacks as she walked down the hall. She was at the door when the bell rang and she swung it open.

"Hi," he said, his gaze sweeping over her from head to foot. "You look nice."

"Thanks," she said. The memory of him promising to come earlier the next time they had a date so he could kiss her before she put on her lipstick popped into her mind. But then she already had it on this time too. And she shouldn't want him to kiss her again.

"Are you ready?" he asked.

"Well, I'm as ready as I'll ever be," she quipped, looking up to meet his gaze.

The brown of his shirt showing through

his open beige trench coat brought out the rusty color of his eyes. She'd always looked to his eyes to tell her when he was serious and when he was teasing her. Now his smile made those eyes sparkle while the corners crinkled a little.

"Come in. I just have to put my coat on," she said, stepping back a little.

He stepped inside the door so she could close it and saw that he wasn't alone.

"You brought Fred," she said, surprised.

Leaning down, she petted Fred and rubbed his ears the way her dogs liked. Jealous, the boys circled Carter, and he reached down to pet them both. They soon deserted him to give their attention to their buddy Fred.

"Yes, and we're in no rush. We're going to a place that doesn't take reservations, but I have a feeling we won't have to wait long." Fred started to rise from his sitting position to play, but Carter tugged on the leash and commanded him to sit, which he did at once.

Reaching into the foyer closet for her coat, she stopped suddenly and turned back to him. "But you have Fred with you."

"Yes, and you can bring Day and Night with you, if you want."

Suspicious, she put her fisted hands on

her hips. "I won't go to your apartment for dinner, Carter. This dinner will be on neutral territory or not at all."

He laughed and held up his hand with the palm toward her like a traffic cop stopping the line of cars. "Nope, dinner is not at my place, though that would be nice. I found a place that will allow you to take your dogs."

Her fists relaxed and her hands slid down as her arms straightened. "But there's no place like that in this town. You can't have dogs in a restaurant unless it's a medical aide. Those are Health Department regulations. This isn't France."

"This one is right here in town, and you can bring your dogs — really."

"Well, you have my curiosity piqued, but I'm leaving the boys home anyway. I don't have the energy to have them with me, not after the day I've had."

He looked at the end of the tiled hall where the kiddie pool sat. The newly rescued puppies were there, but the trio of puppies she'd had for several weeks was nowhere in sight.

"Hey, where are the three little puppies I helped with?"

She smiled. "They're now on their way to good homes. Sam took them after the parade," she said proudly. "It's always a bittersweet time for me. I love caring for them and I hate to see them go. On the other hand, I can't keep them or deny them a good life with a new family. Besides, the new ones are more than enough to handle."

"I didn't realize the trio would be gone."

"Well, we got so many families who volunteered to take one that Sam decided to take them today and give them out tomorrow. It might be easier on families with kids to welcome them on a weekend day instead of a school day."

"On the other hand, that would be worth skipping school to do it on a weekday," Carter replied with a chuckle.

"That's what he's afraid they'll think. So now they'll be happy to go to school Monday to share the tales of getting one of the puppies that was in the parade."

"That was quite a parade," Carter put in. "You're to be congratulated."

With his help, Terri slipped into her coat. Leaning closer, he lifted out the collar that had been caught inside the shoulder. His warm fingers touched her neck and shivers traveled down her back. "Thank you," she said in a voice that almost failed her.

"The new puppies are doing okay?"

"I think we got them just in time."

"How's their mother doing?"

"Um . . . she didn't make it. I guess it happens a lot that way."

"Oh, I'm sorry," he said softly.

Looking at him, she could easily believe that he was truly sorry. That was fine and good, but for all the people who mistreated their dogs, sorry wasn't nearly good enough.

Grabbing her shoulder bag from the table, she fastened the mesh gate across the hallway to isolate the kiddie pool from the rest. "The puppies are too weak for Night and Day to play with."

Walking ahead of Carter, she opened the front door and called a good-bye to the boys. At his pickup she waited while he put Fred in the protective cage he had seat-belted onto the backseat of his truck. In case of an accident, he would be safer in there.

Opening the passenger door for her, he said, "Don't worry. I wiped off the seats. They get pretty dusty at construction sites."

"The new project is starting?" she asked, genuinely interested though she knew she shouldn't be. Breaking up with him would be even harder if she knew what he was do-ing and where he would be working.

"It's close. We're at the surveying stage and driving in stakes like crazy," he said with a laugh. "They'll start digging soon. I still have a little more work on the first

Riverside to do before that, though, before we can begin the second Riverside."

Surprising her, he drove directly to the first Riverside. Parking at the end near her shop, he jumped out and came around to her door. Instead of waiting for him, she had already exited the truck when he got there. She waited as he let Fred out. Holding his leash, he ordered Fred to heel and then took Terri's elbow and steered her toward the walkway.

"Where are we going?"

"We're going to the restaurant of course," he answered.

"But the only one open after the stores close on Saturday night is Pierre's."

"Right — I hear the food is good too."

"But what about Fred?" she asked.

"He can come too."

"I thought dogs weren't permitted on the walkway."

"It seems Bob changed his mind and never put up the signs."

As they walked around the curved walk and arrived at Pierre's, Terri stopped. She could see tables and chairs set out on the walkway next to the lawn that sloped to the river. Tall propane heaters warmed and lit the area as waiters and waitresses in black scurried back and forth from inside the restaurant.

"If you don't want to sit out here, Fred will wait in the truck," Carter said softly. "He'll be fine there on a cool evening like this."

Looking again at the tables, she could see several diners had dogs beside them. One had her tiny pet on her lap. "This all looks very French," she said.

"Are you game to dine with Fred outside, or should we sit inside without the dog?"

Smiling, she looked up at Carter and met his gaze. "Fred would never forgive me if I was responsible for sending him back to the truck." And tonight might be the last time she would see Fred, she thought. "Let's eat outside together."

They were seated at a linen-covered table by the lawn, and Fred made himself comfortable on the grass by Carter's chair as he had thousands of times at the side of the blind person he had aided during his active service years.

Terri had imagined that the evening would be awkward. She thought she really shouldn't have come, but she couldn't stay away. They put in their orders and somehow got into a conversation about the river.

"My dad loved to fish in the river just below the dam," Carter told her.

"I've never been fishing," she had to admit.

"What did you say?" he asked, feigning horror.

She shrugged. "We were city folk who could never afford a cottage on this or any river or lake. With no brothers to encourage fishing, I never learned."

"Well, we have to remedy that. I'll take you out fishing next spring when the season opens. And then you're in for a treat. I'll fix them myself for dinner. You haven't tasted good fried catfish until you've tasted mine."

She laughed, though suddenly she felt very sad. Shaking her head, she looked down at her napkin. The waiter arrived with their salads and saved her from commenting, but she knew there would be no fishing trip or dinner together next spring. Unless the publicity from the parade worked a miracle, she would be working seven days a week to get a new store up and running at some other location. Or, heaven forbid, she might be working in an office somewhere and going home to an empty apartment. She shook her head to clear it and concentrated on her salad. "Oh, look. There's watercress in here — yum."

"I love watching you eat salads," he said softly. "You really do enjoy them."

"They're one of nature's treats," she agreed. "I'm probably part rabbit."

He laughed softly. "And I love your sense of humor."

She set down her fork and patted her mouth. "Carter, please don't. I agreed to meet with you tonight because you said you had something important to tell me and something to show me. That's why I'm here. I'm not here to listen to what you . . . like about me."

"Point taken — I'll try to keep what I love about you to myself for the time being," he agreed.

She sighed. "What did you want to show me, Carter?"

"Oh, it's in the truck. I didn't want to disrupt our dinner together. I'll show it to you afterwards."

"But I agreed to go to dinner with you only to see whatever it was that was so important to show me. Why didn't you bring it with you to the restaurant?"

He slid his hand across the table and captured hers before she could pull it away. Holding it in his, he stroked the back with his thumb. "Terri, I promise you that I do have something very important to show you, but won't you please wait until after dinner to see it? Right now, I hoped we could enjoy each other's company without our thoughts even going near the reason why we haven't been together lately. I enjoy being with you, Terri. I've missed being with you." He grinned suddenly. "Fred missed you."

They both glanced down beside the table to see Fred was sound asleep. He didn't even wiggle at hearing his name.

"So unless this is making you too uncomfortable to enjoy your dinner, let's just eat and talk about the weather if we must — okay?"

Did she enjoy being with him? Of course she did. She'd been falling in love with him for weeks. However, that did not erase how angry she was that he had misled her about who he was.

But maybe he was right. They were adults. Certainly they could manage to be mature and put aside their differences long enough to eat a dinner together. She didn't want either of them to get an ulcer, that's for sure.

But they didn't have to hold hands while they ate, she decided.

She nodded and pulled her hand free. Swallowing hard, she reached for her fork. Her mind raced to think of something neutral that they could talk about — other than the weather.

Chapter Thirteen

"I take it Sam hasn't called again," Carter said after a few moments of silence.

"No, either he hasn't been overloaded with dogs or they haven't had to rescue many more. I hope it's the latter." She snorted a laugh. "I still have my hands full with the last ones you helped to rescue. But I think the fact that they're little imps is a good sign. They get more energetic each day."

Terri and Carter did manage to keep the conversation light all the way through dinner. It hadn't been all that hard. Carter always had been easy to talk to. She couldn't remember a time when she hadn't enjoyed herself when they were together. And that made the whole frustrating situation even sadder.

They declined a dessert and had just coffee instead. Pierre came out as they finished and thanked her again for organizing the parade and bringing in so many customers. He embarrassed her by letting the other people there with dogs know that it was thanks to her tireless efforts in keeping dogs allowed on the walkway.

"I didn't know that they had decided not to ban them," she said.

"Oh, yes. I hear the rumor for no dogs, and I call M&S. They say no dogs are allowed anytime now." Pierre was called back to the kitchen and couldn't say more.

Terri looked to Carter for an explanation, but he was getting out his credit card to give the waiter. Not allowing her to split the bill, Carter paid for both dinners. Rising from their table after he'd signed the receipt, Fred quickly assumed the heel position without Carter saying a word. He picked up the leash and they strolled slowly down the walkway toward her shop on the end. His truck was parked just beyond the building.

"Fred is really an amazing animal," she allowed. "You seem to have done it all right with him behaving as well as he does."

He captured her hand in his and wouldn't let it go when she tried to tug it loose. "I wish I had done it all right with you," he said softly.

"Carter, I really don't think . . ."

"I know," he said, cutting her off. "Do you

272

have your shop key on you?" he asked as they rounded the end of the building and neared the truck.

"Sure I do. It's always on my key ring."

"I hoped it would be." Opening the truck door, he pulled out a metal tube from behind the seat. "Can we look at what I brought in there?"

"Sure, I suppose so."

They walked over to the rear door and Terri unlocked it. Stepping inside, she entered her code in the security system to temporarily shut it off. Closing the door after Carter had entered, she locked it and dropped her keys back into her bag. Low-level lights that she kept on twenty-four hours a day lit their way through the kitchen and into the showroom. All the while she noticed that he was looking around and apparently not finding what he was looking for.

"What are you looking for?"

"I need a wide space. How about your desk in the office? Is it as full of stuff as the counter here?"

She laughed. "No, with all that was going on today, the shop is a work in progress until we can get it back to normal again on Monday. Come on. I do straighten up my office once in a while."

Leading the way into her office, she flipped on the light. Walking around to her chair, she felt better for having put the desk between her and Carter. She dropped her purse on the chair and turned to him. He was unscrewing the end of the tube and proceeded to pull out blueprints. Laying them on the desk he weighted the corners down with her pencil mug and the phone. She pulled a stapler from her drawer for the third corner and put her shoulder bag on the fourth. He flipped on her desk lamp that illuminated the blueprints and made a strong contrast to the dimly lit space around them.

Now that she could see the drawings more clearly, she thought it looked like her shop. She could see the office in which they stood and the dog run that allowed Night and Day to go from there to an area on the sales room floor. There they could see people but not get into trouble.

"What is it? It's close to the floor plan of this shop, but this is all different," she said, waving a hand over the end of the drawing.

He moved around to her side of the desk so he didn't have to view it upside down. She didn't think about moving away to put more space between them. Their shoulders touched as they bent over the plans.

"Terri, this is the floor plan for the alter-
ation to your shop to give you a main
entrance in the rear. I've tried to plan it
exactly like you wanted it — the way you
told me at our last dinner together. Here's
the new entrance," he said, pointing to it.
"You have a nice grassy area here, so you'll
have to put one of those doggybag dispens-
ers out there too," he said with a laugh.
"Ugh, that gives a restaurant *doggie bag* a
whole new meaning."

But Terri wasn't laughing at his play on
words. She was trying to understand.

"Here's the window where kids, and
adults too, for that matter, can watch Tom
bake up all those doggy treats. He said he's
going to like having an audience off and on."

Terri jerked her head up. "You talked to
him about this?"

"Yes, and I talked to Sue as well."

"But you didn't talk to me?"

He took a deep breath and expelled it
slowly. "Well, we have talked, in that you
talked about it at our dinner. Until I knew
what was going to happen, I didn't want to
get your hopes up. I couldn't bear to see
you unhappy and upset again."

"So you talked to them instead."

"Yes, I wanted to find out how you used
the space — where the best placement of

the new window was, where the door into the kitchen should be so it would present the least interference with how you use the space, that sort of thing."

Terri wiped her face with her hands and tried to make sense of this all. "You didn't want to see me upset again and yet you're showing me these plans now?"

"Yes, and I'm trying to tell you that M&S is going to build the addition for you." He grasped her shoulders and turned her toward him. "And I'm telling you that the eviction notice, with which I swear I had no involvement or even any knowledge until well after the fact, is rescinded if this plan is agreeable with you. And if it's not right, I'll fix it until it is right."

"I'm not evicted?" she managed to ask past the lump that grew in her throat.

"No, Bob has finally agreed with me. You do not have to move out of your space at Riverside."

The blood seeped out of her head and Terri thought she would faint. His strong hands held her firmly, and she couldn't look away from his face. She looked deep into his eyes, but she didn't see any of the deception that she somehow expected to see there. But he wouldn't do that — not Carter.

"But your partner said no one wanted us here. He said the other store owners complained about us."

"Yes, well, I'm sorry about that. It turned out to be a very vocal minority, and that minority is now very vocal in support of your store. I don't know if you have figured it out yet, but except for a couple Christmas-shopping days last winter, the number of people who came to Riverside for your parade set a record. And lots of them stayed to shop and eat meals and snacks."

"It was a bigger crowd than I expected," she said numbly. "It all worked out quite well, I think."

"In the face of those numbers and all the calls we were getting in your support, Bob had to change his mind. One more article in the paper and he would be nicknamed Scrooge." He snorted a laugh. "And I didn't give him a choice to do anything but allow you to stay."

"And K-Nine Treats can stay the way it is?"

"It can stay with the new entrance to make it even better. You're not a liability to Riverside — you're a big asset. And an article in Monday's paper will say that."

Tears of joy rolled down her cheeks.

"Thank you, Carter."

He tugged on her shoulders to draw her close against his chest. "Aw, honey, I . . ."

Raising her hands to stop him, she pushed away. "So once you've told me that I'm not evicted, you think I'm going to be so very grateful that I will fall into your arms. Is that it?"

He frowned. "Just a minute here. Don't tell me you don't like being in my arms because I won't believe you," he retorted.

"Well, what about honesty and truth? What about trust? What about the fact you were part owner in M&S and never told me? Now I finally know the truth, no thanks to you, and I'm suddenly supposed to go back to where we were?"

"Terri, I've said I had nothing to do with the eviction."

"Then why didn't you tell me where you worked?"

His shoulders slumped and he stepped back. "I didn't think you'd believe I had nothing to do with it. I was afraid to tell you back then."

"Why is that? Do you think I couldn't understand the ways of big business that would separate duties so you couldn't know all of what Bob did? Or maybe you just thought I was so stupid that you could lead mc on as long as possible before I happened to find out that you did have a part in it?"

"Terri, no — I knew from the moment we met that you were both bright and beautiful. At first you didn't tell me you owned this shop. You just said you worked here. Well, I didn't mention that I owned part of the business because I just couldn't bear the thought of losing you."

"Why go to all this trouble?" she demanded, gesturing toward the drawings.

"Because I love you," he said softly.

Terri gasped.

"And I would be devastated if I lost you," he added. "I kept at Bob until he relented so you could stay here. And I'd do it all again and more before I'd let you go. But I will never try to hide the complete truth from you again, never."

Terri blinked at the tears that flowed freely down her cheeks. She couldn't believe what she was hearing and raised her trembling hands to his shoulders. "You love me?"

"I love you with all my heart, and if I can't convince you of that tonight, I'll try again tomorrow and the days after that until you see that I'm sincere."

Rising on her toes, she threw her arms around his neck and hugged him. "Oh, Carter, I have wanted so badly to believe in you.

I didn't see how I could be so wrong about the wonderful kind of man you are, and now I know that I wasn't. Oh, I love you for what you've done for me."

He wrapped his arms around her, holding her against his chest. "I'm glad, but that's not exactly the way I wanted to hear you say that."

Sniffling, she tipped her head up to meet his gaze. "What do you mean? I believe that you had nothing to do with the rental decisions that got me in line to be evicted. And I know how hard you worked to figure out a way to save the shop for me and make your partner agree to it."

"It's natural to want to help you, honey."

"Oh, Carter, do you really love me?"

"Tell me you're not doubting me already." Pulling her close, his lips covered hers. They pressed and nipped playfully. He caught her lower lip between his and tugged on it only to release it and kiss her again more firmly.

A while later when the kiss ended, he asked, "Oh, honey, can you doubt it now?"

She shook her head. "I never could doubt your love again. And I love you too."

"But do you love me *only* for what I did to help you?"

"No way — I've been falling in love with you for weeks. And, much to my dismay, I still loved you even when I thought you were two-faced."

"That's what I wanted to hear." He hugged her.

"You wanted to hear that I thought you were two-faced?" she asked with a laugh.

"No, I wanted to hear that you loved me no matter what. But I was willing to be patient and wait to hear you say it," he added.

"You would have waited?"

"Sure," he said with a grin. "As well as our dogs get along, I just knew there had to be a future together for us."

EPILOGUE

Four months later

Balancing it in her bathtub, Terri finished scrubbing the toddler swimming pool that had been home to four spaniel puppies. She turned the handheld shower on it to rinse away the cleanser.

Carter held the shower curtain to the side and laughed. "You're as wet as the pool," he told her.

"You're not exactly dry yourself."

Propping the pool against the back of the shower, they left it to dry.

"That's the last of it. Once it's dry, I lean it against the wall in the big hall closet until I need it again," she explained as they returned to the kitchen.

"There, the last of the little bottles are in plastic bags and packed." He alternately folded in the flaps on the box and tapped the top. "Where do you want this?"

"It goes in the closet to hold the pool in

place after it's dry."

"You have this all down to a science."

"In an apartment this small, I have to pack things away efficiently." She washed her hands. "Would you want some hot chocolate?"

"I'd love some. Then you can see what I brought to show you."

She smiled. "What did you bring me?"

"Get to work, my love. Make that hot chocolate, and then you'll find out."

Pulling out a pan, she poured in the milk and set it to heat on the stove. Opening packets of chocolate and sugar mix, she sprinkled them in and stirred.

"Let me think now. When you came in, all you had in your hands was a blueprint case." She shrugged. "Since you came by on your way home from the office, I thought you were just taking work home with you."

"Are you trying to wheedle more information out of me?"

She laughed and poured the warm drink into two mugs. "Where do you want to drink it?"

"How about here at the kitchen table?"

His answer surprised her. "Sure," she said as she set the mugs on the table.

He turned and exited the room for a minute or so. Coming right back, he held the blueprint tube under one arm as he unscrewed the lid.

"Now will you tell me what you've got in there?" she asked, pushing their mugs aside.

"Huh, it's a set of blueprints. Go figure," he jested.

Spreading them out on the table, he accepted her help when she got four cans of dog food to hold down the corners.

"Okay, come around here," he said, his arm out to wrap around her when she reached his side.

Resting her hands on the edge of the table, she leaned over and studied the blueprint. "Whatever it is, it has a lot of rooms," she said.

It wasn't until she looked at the title box in the lower corner that she knew what she was looking at. Straightening, she met his grinning gaze.

"It's an apartment in the new building at Riverside Two."

"Yes, and if you like it, it's our apartment in the new building at Riverside Two. I've designed it just for us."

Leaning over the plans again, he pulled a pen from his pocket and used it as a pointer to explain. "It's in the corner overlooking the dam, and on the top floor."

He looked at her and frowned. "I hope

you're not afraid of heights."

She had to laugh. "No I'm not, not at all. I bet the view will be spectacular."

"They'll be even better than the one from my office."

She groaned. "Go on. Go on. What else is there?"

"The entry hall leads to the living room. The dining room's here beyond the kitchen-family room that has its own eating area."

"Oh, Carter, it's beautiful."

"Here's our bedroom, and these two are for guests." He looked at her and tucked a loose curl behind her ear. "Or they could be for our children."

"These plans are wonderful," she said softly, tipping her head up to meet his lips with hers.

Eventually looking back at the drawing, she was puzzled. "But what's this space back here behind the kitchen? Is it another bedroom? I see it has its own bathroom like the others."

"That's for your babies," he said with a grin.

"But you said these rooms were for our children," she countered, pointing to the two bedrooms off the main hall.

"This other room is for your four-legged babies."

She looked at the drawings and then flung her arms around his neck and hugged him. "Then you don't mind that I want to keep on volunteering after we're married?"

"That would be like stopping you from being you. I love you, Terri, and what you do, namely rescuing puppies, is part of what makes you who you are."

She kissed his ear. "I'm very glad you caught me that day in the park when Night and Day tripped me up."

Separating a little, he smiled. "I want to kiss you so much, but if I do now, I'll forget to tell you that the room for the puppies is even insulated so their barking won't bother the neighbors or wake our children."

"You think of everything."

"I don't know. Most of the time, I'm thinking of you."

"I love you so much." She grinned suddenly. "Okay, now," she said, following the curve of his ear with her fingertip.

"Now what, my love?"

"Now that you've told me, you can kiss me."

The employees of Thorndike Press hope you have enjoyed this Large Print book. All our Thorndike, Wheeler, and Kennebec Large Print titles are designed for easy reading, and all our books are made to last. Other Thorndike Press Large Print books are available at your library, through selected bookstores, or directly from us.

For information about titles, please call:
(800) 223-1244

or visit our Web site at:
http://gale.cengage.com/thorndike

To share your comments, please write:
Publisher
Thorndike Press
10 Water St., Suite 310
Waterville, ME 04901